vol.2___

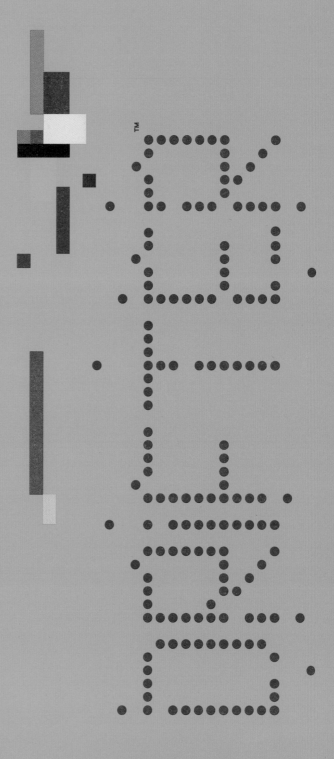

IMAGECOMICS.COM
ISBN: 978-1-63215-501-6

DRIFTER VOL 2. First Printing. December 2015. Published by Image Comics, Inc. Office of publication: 2001 Center Street, Sixth Floor, Berkeley, CA
94704. Copyright © 2015 Againdemon, LLC & Nicolas Klein. All rights reserved. DRIFTER™ (including all prominent characters featured herein), its logo
and all character likenesses are trademarks of Againdemon, LLC & Nicolas Klein, unless otherwise noted. Image Comics® and its logos are registered
trademarks of Image Comics, Inc. No part of this publication may be reproduced or transmitted, in any form or by any means (except short excerpts for
review purposes) without the express written permission of Againdemon, LLC, Nicolas Klein, or Image Comics, Inc. All names, characters, events, and
locales in this publication are entirely fictional. Any resemblance to actual persons (living or dead), events, or places, without satire intent, is coincidental.
First printed in single magazine format as DRIFTER #6-9 by Image Comics, Inc. Printed in the USA. For information regarding the CPSIA on this printed
material call: 203-595-3636 and provide reference #RICH-656562.
Representation: Law Offices of Harris M. Miller II, P.C.

Drifter Volume 02
Originally published as DRIFTER #6-9

Script: Ivan Brandon
Full color art and cover: Nic Klein
Lettering: Clem Robins
Logo and design: Tom Muller
Editor: Sebastian Girner
Special thanks to Kristyn Ferretti
Wind Beneath Our Wings: Kieron Dwyer

Original cover artists: Nic Klein, Eduardo Risso,
Tom Muller, Daniel Krall, and Paul Azaceta

CHAPTER 6
TRACK THE STARS

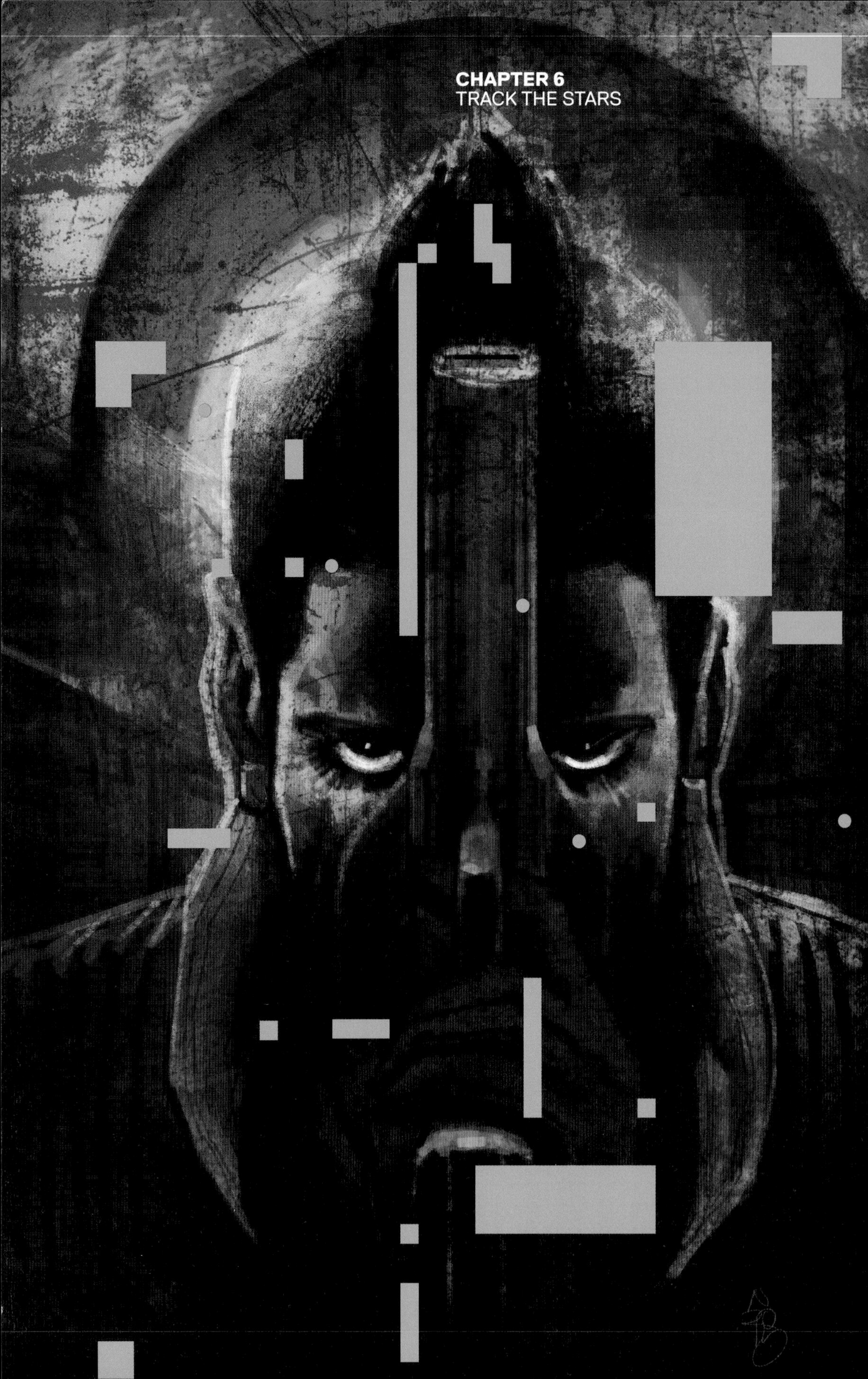

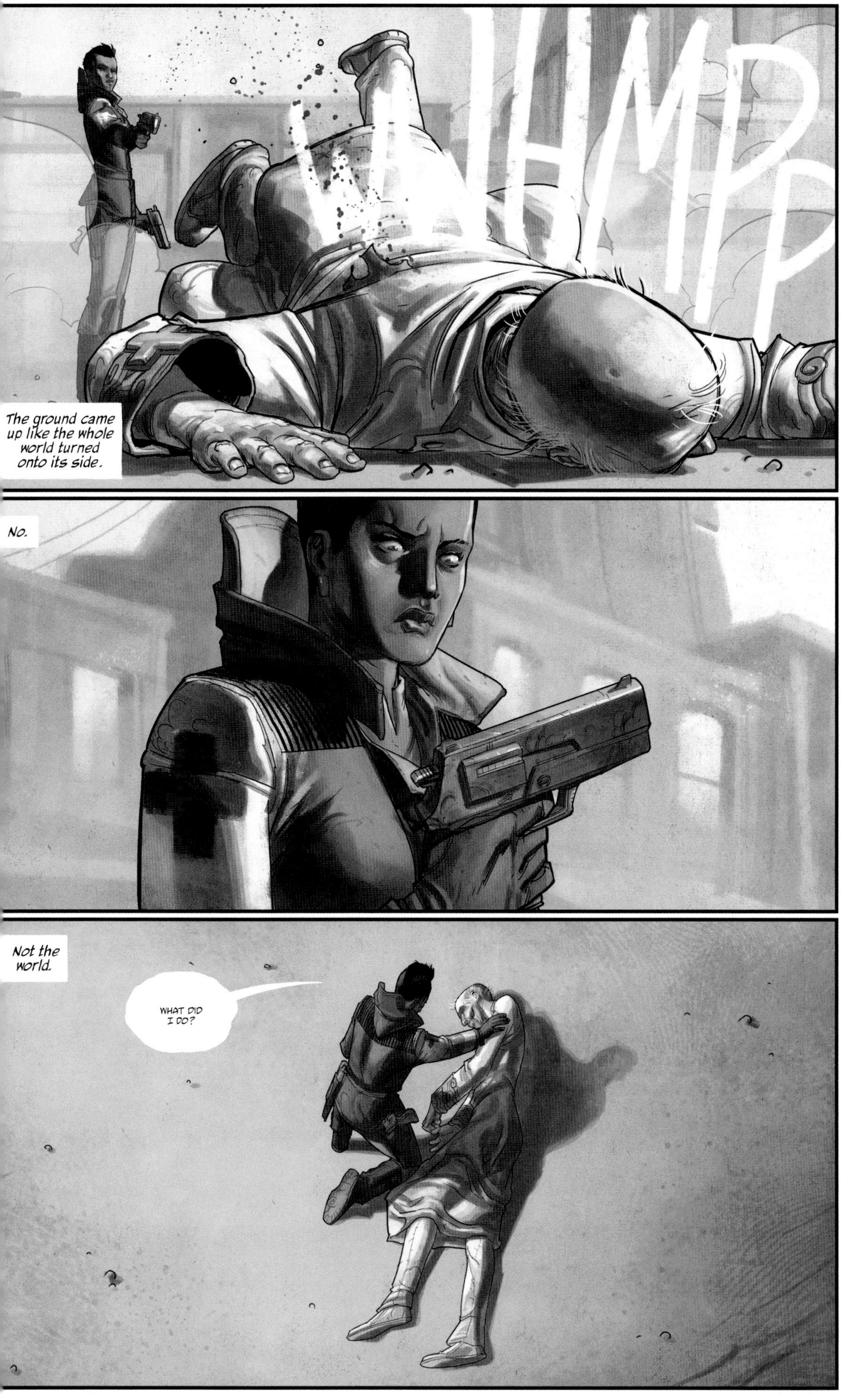
WHUMPP
The ground came up like the whole world turned onto its side.
No.
Not the world.
WHAT DID I DO?

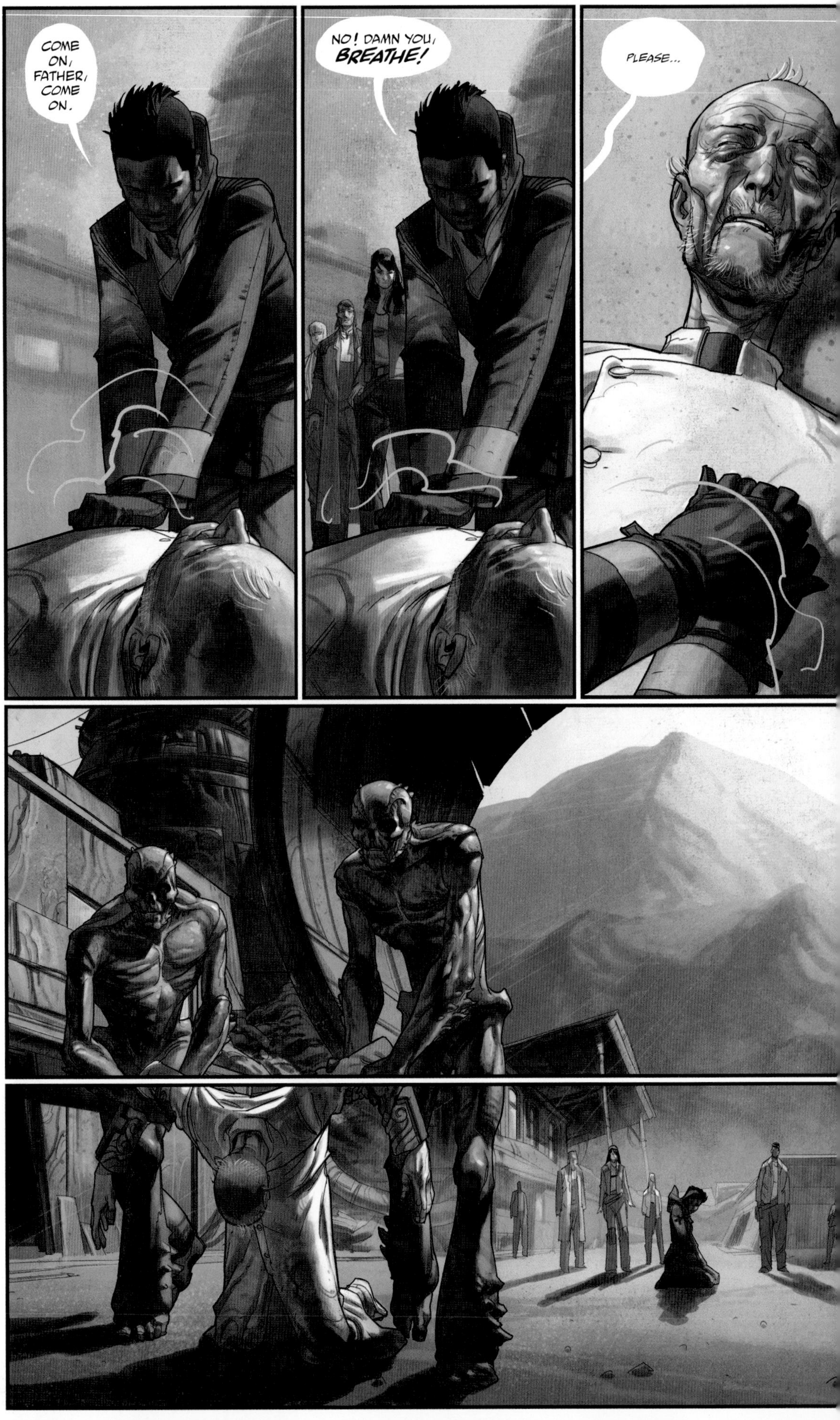
COME ON, FATHER, COME ON.
NO! DAMN YOU, BREATHE!
PLEASE...

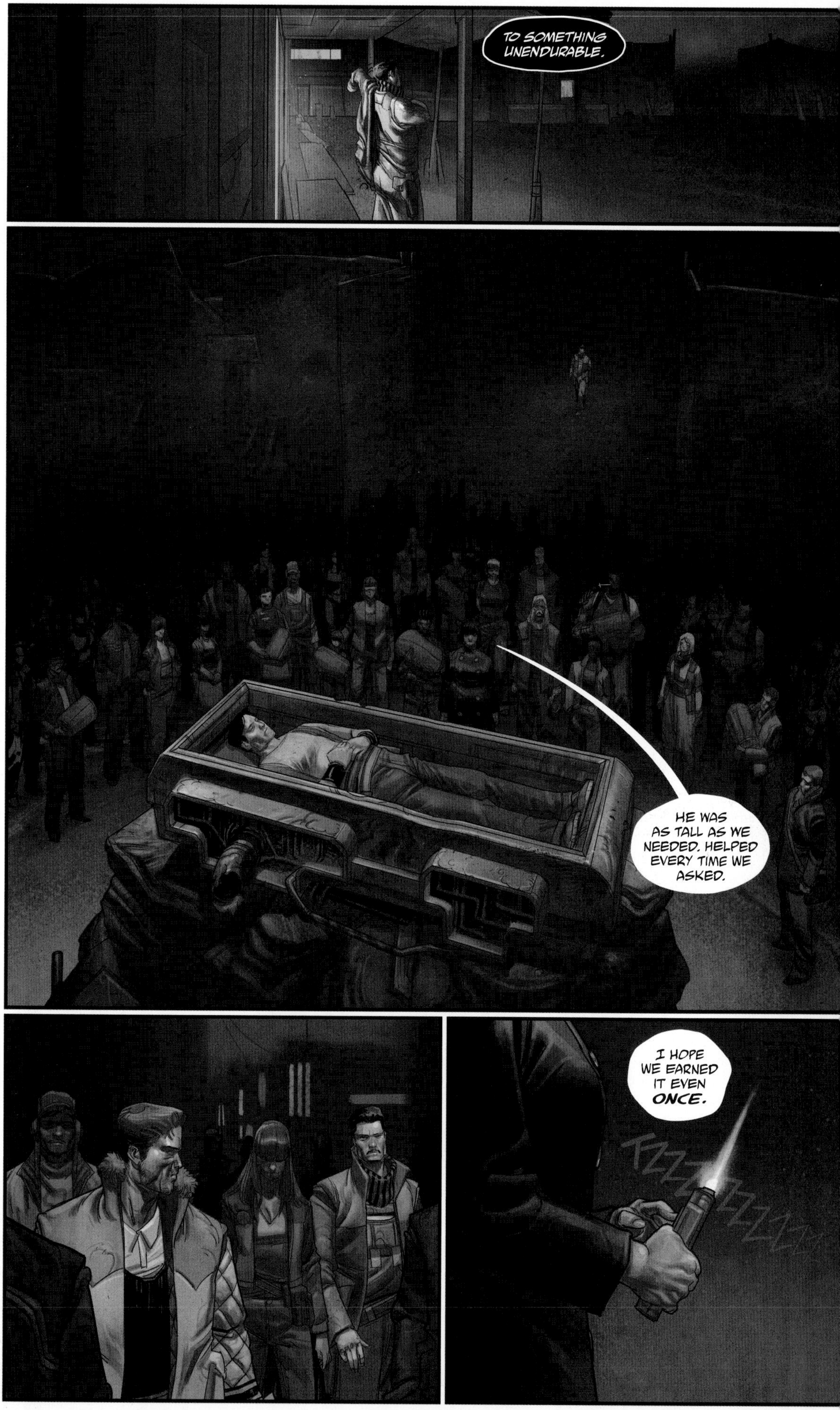
TO SOMETHING UNENDURABLE.
HE WAS AS TALL AS WE NEEDED. HELPED EVERY TIME WE ASKED.
I HOPE WE EARNED IT EVEN ONCE.
TZZZZZZZZZ

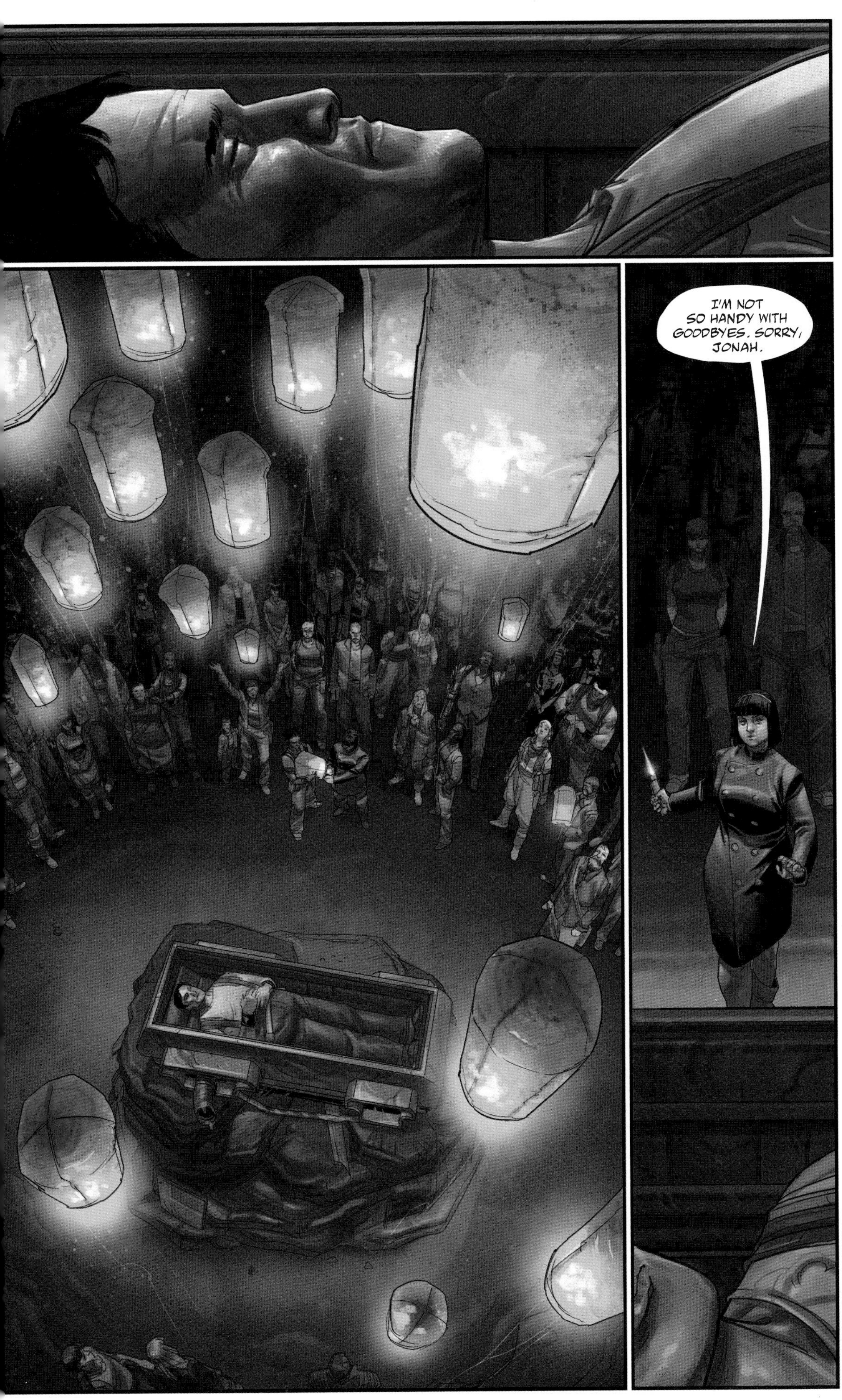
I'M NOT SO HANDY WITH GOODBYES. SORRY, JONAH.

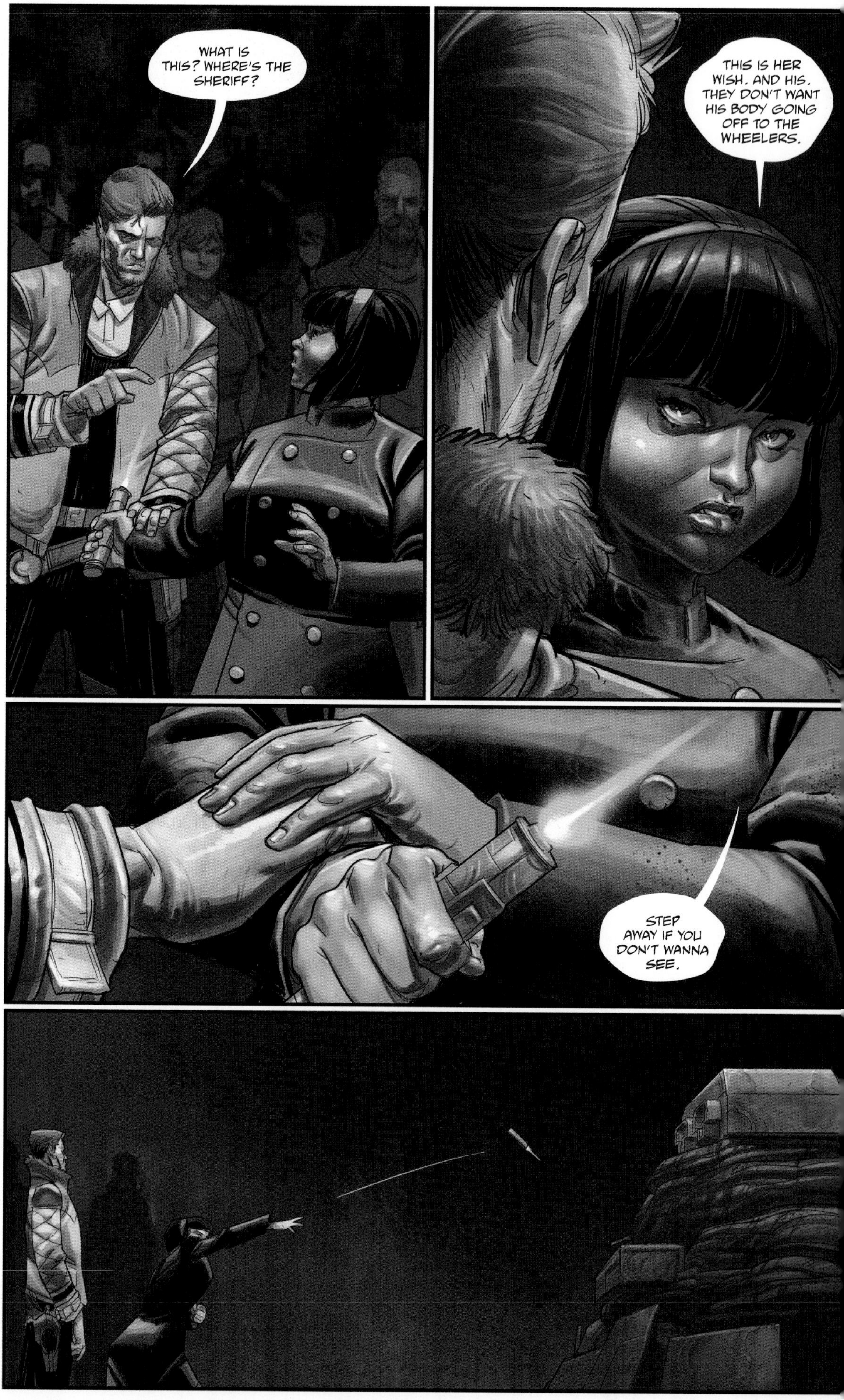
WHAT IS THIS? WHERE'S THE SHERIFF?
THIS IS HER WISH. AND HIS. THEY DON'T WANT HIS BODY GOING OFF TO THE WHEELERS.
STEP AWAY IF YOU DON'T WANNA SEE.

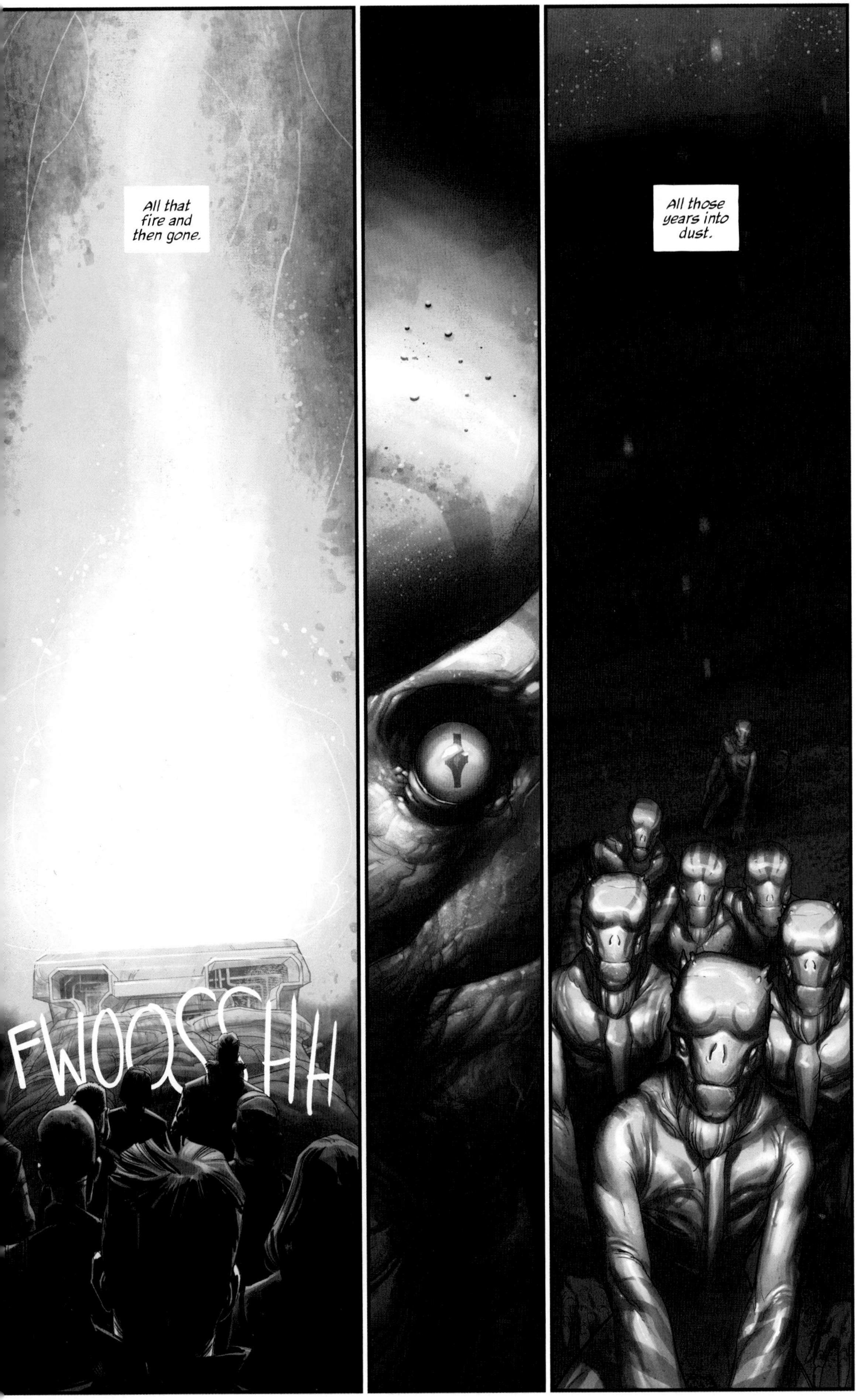
All that fire and then gone.
FWOOSCHH
All those years into dust.

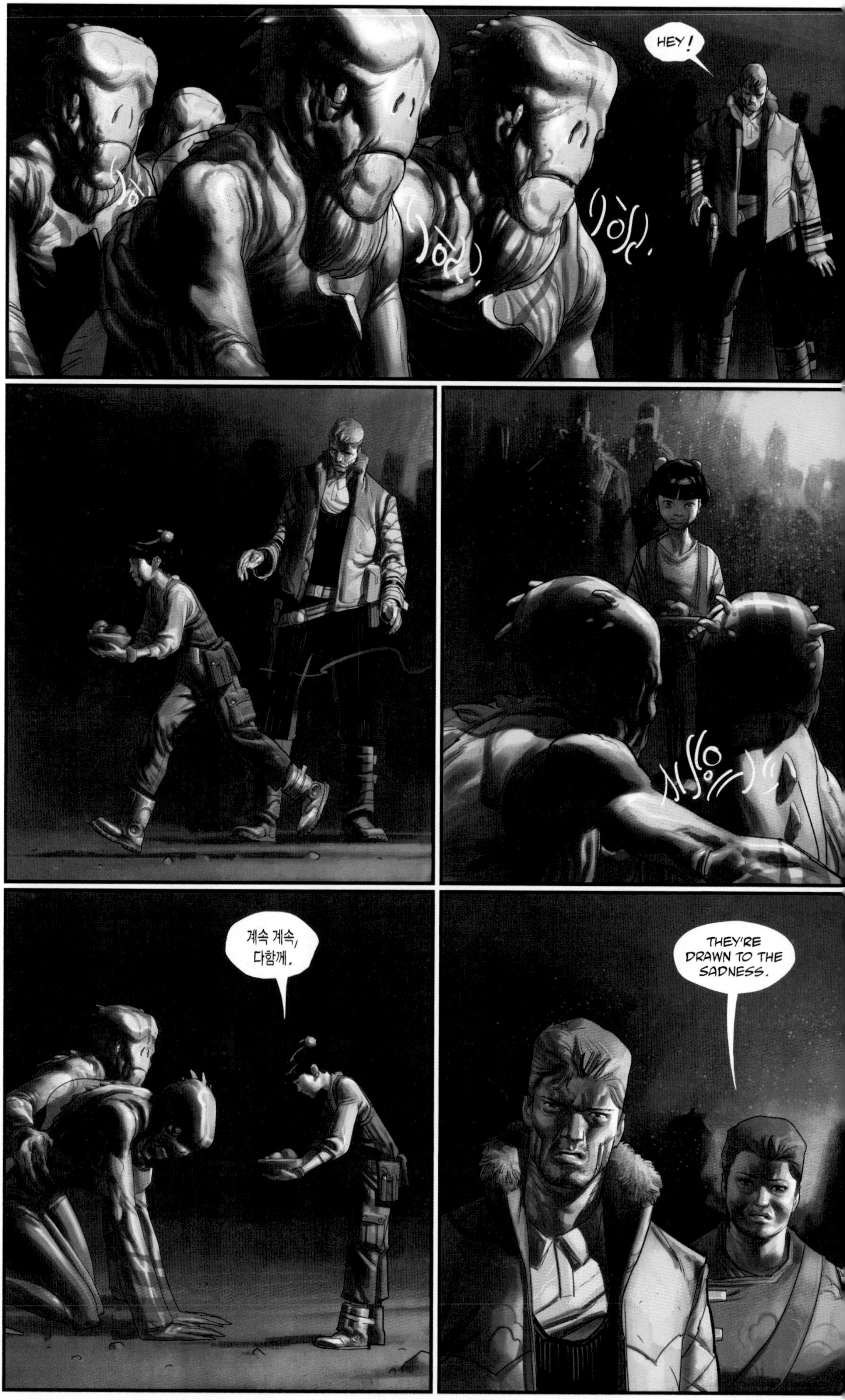
HEY!
계속 계속,
다함께.
THEY'RE DRAWN TO THE SADNESS.

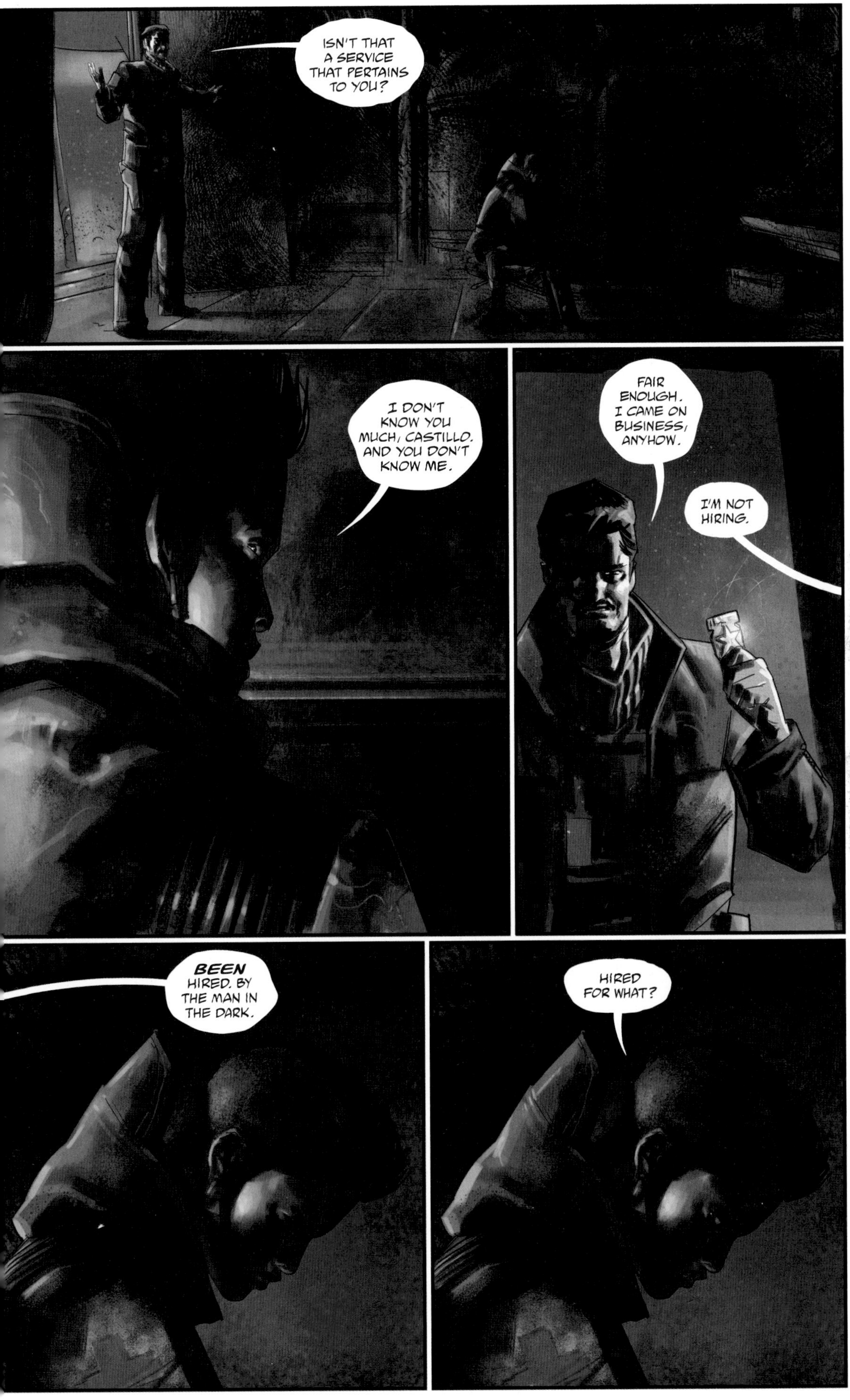
ISN'T THAT A SERVICE THAT PERTAINS TO YOU?
I DON'T KNOW YOU MUCH, CASTILLO. AND YOU DON'T KNOW ME.
FAIR ENOUGH. I CAME ON BUSINESS, ANYHOW.
I'M NOT HIRING.
BEEN HIRED. BY THE MAN IN THE DARK.
HIRED FOR WHAT?

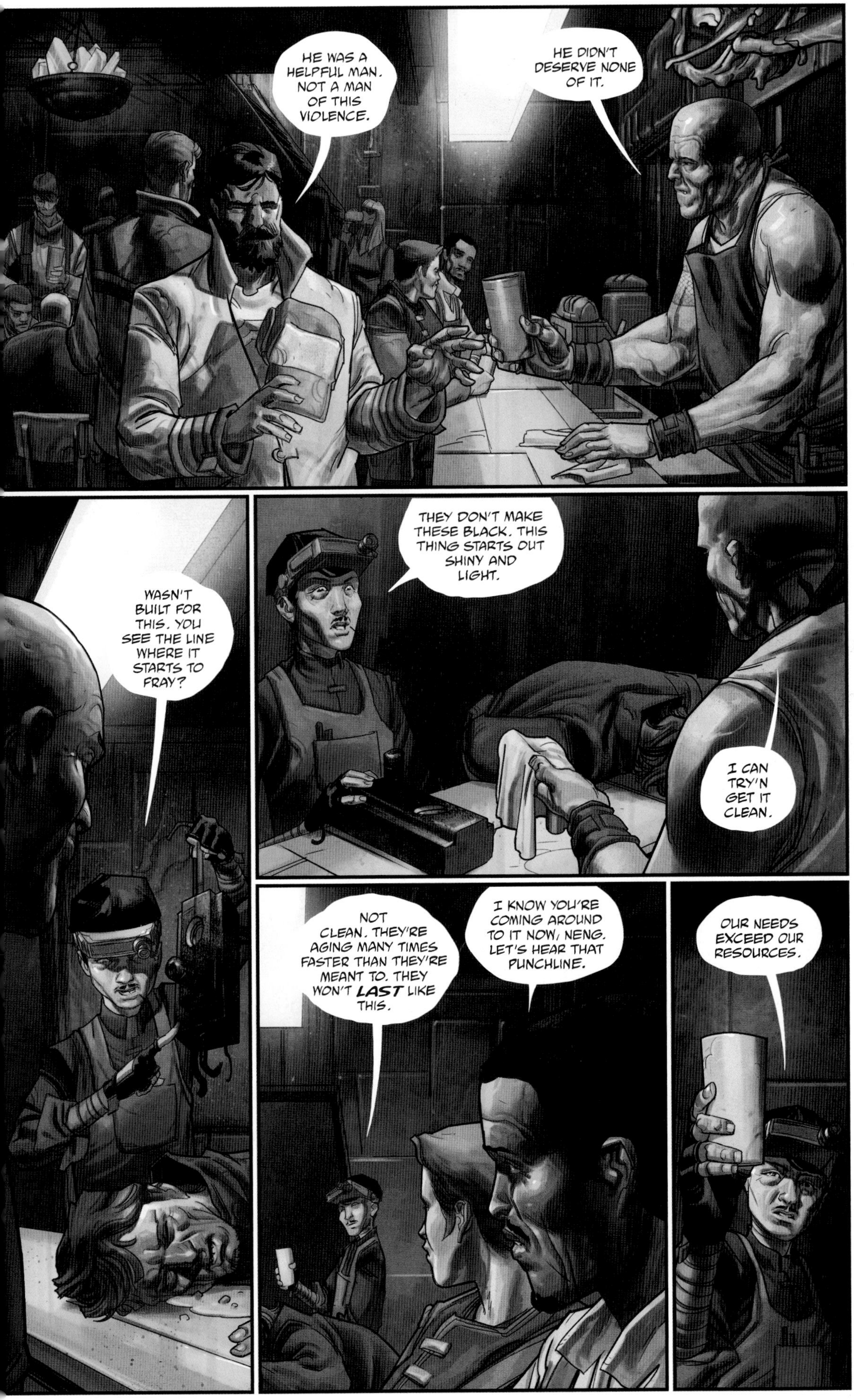
HE WAS A HELPFUL MAN. NOT A MAN OF THIS VIOLENCE.
HE DIDN'T DESERVE NONE OF IT.
WASN'T BUILT FOR THIS. YOU SEE THE LINE WHERE IT STARTS TO FRAY?
THEY DON'T MAKE THESE BLACK. THIS THING STARTS OUT SHINY AND LIGHT.
I CAN TRY'N GET IT CLEAN.
NOT CLEAN. THEY'RE AGING MANY TIMES FASTER THAN THEY'RE MEANT TO. THEY WON'T LAST LIKE THIS.
I KNOW YOU'RE COMING AROUND TO IT NOW, NENG. LET'S HEAR THAT PUNCHLINE.
OUR NEEDS EXCEED OUR RESOURCES.

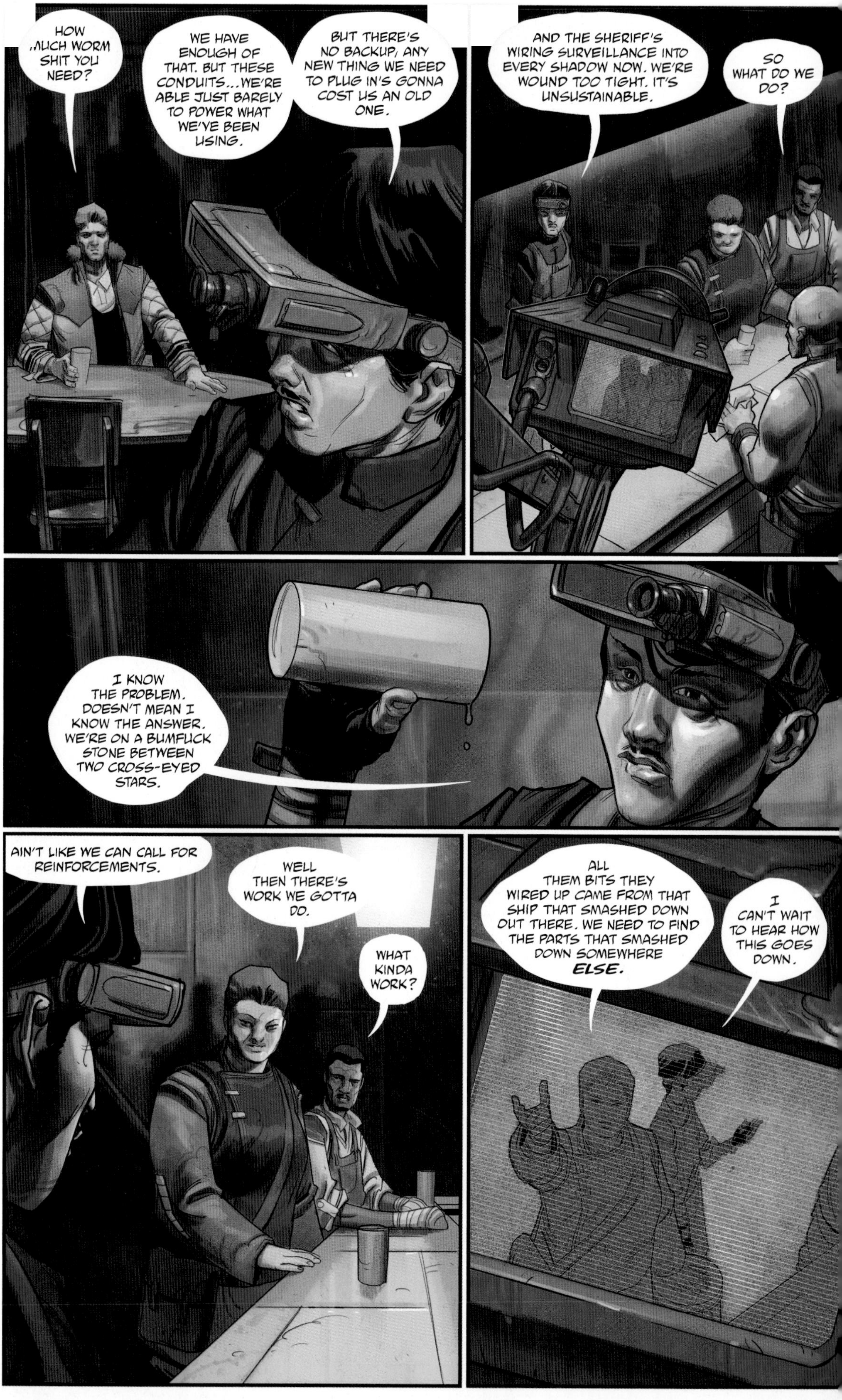
HOW MUCH WORM SHIT YOU NEED?
WE HAVE ENOUGH OF THAT. BUT THESE CONDUITS... WE'RE ABLE JUST BARELY TO POWER WHAT WE'VE BEEN USING.
BUT THERE'S NO BACKUP; ANY NEW THING WE NEED TO PLUG IN'S GONNA COST US AN OLD ONE.
AND THE SHERIFF'S WIRING SURVEILLANCE INTO EVERY SHADOW NOW. WE'RE WOUND TOO TIGHT. IT'S UNSUSTAINABLE.
SO WHAT DO WE DO?
I KNOW THE PROBLEM. DOESN'T MEAN I KNOW THE ANSWER. WE'RE ON A BUMFUCK STONE BETWEEN TWO CROSS-EYED STARS.
AIN'T LIKE WE CAN CALL FOR REINFORCEMENTS.
WELL THEN THERE'S WORK WE GOTTA DO.
WHAT KINDA WORK?
ALL THEM BITS THEY WIRED UP CAME FROM THAT SHIP THAT SMASHED DOWN OUT THERE. WE NEED TO FIND THE PARTS THAT SMASHED DOWN SOMEWHERE ELSE.
I CAN'T WAIT TO HEAR HOW THIS GOES DOWN.

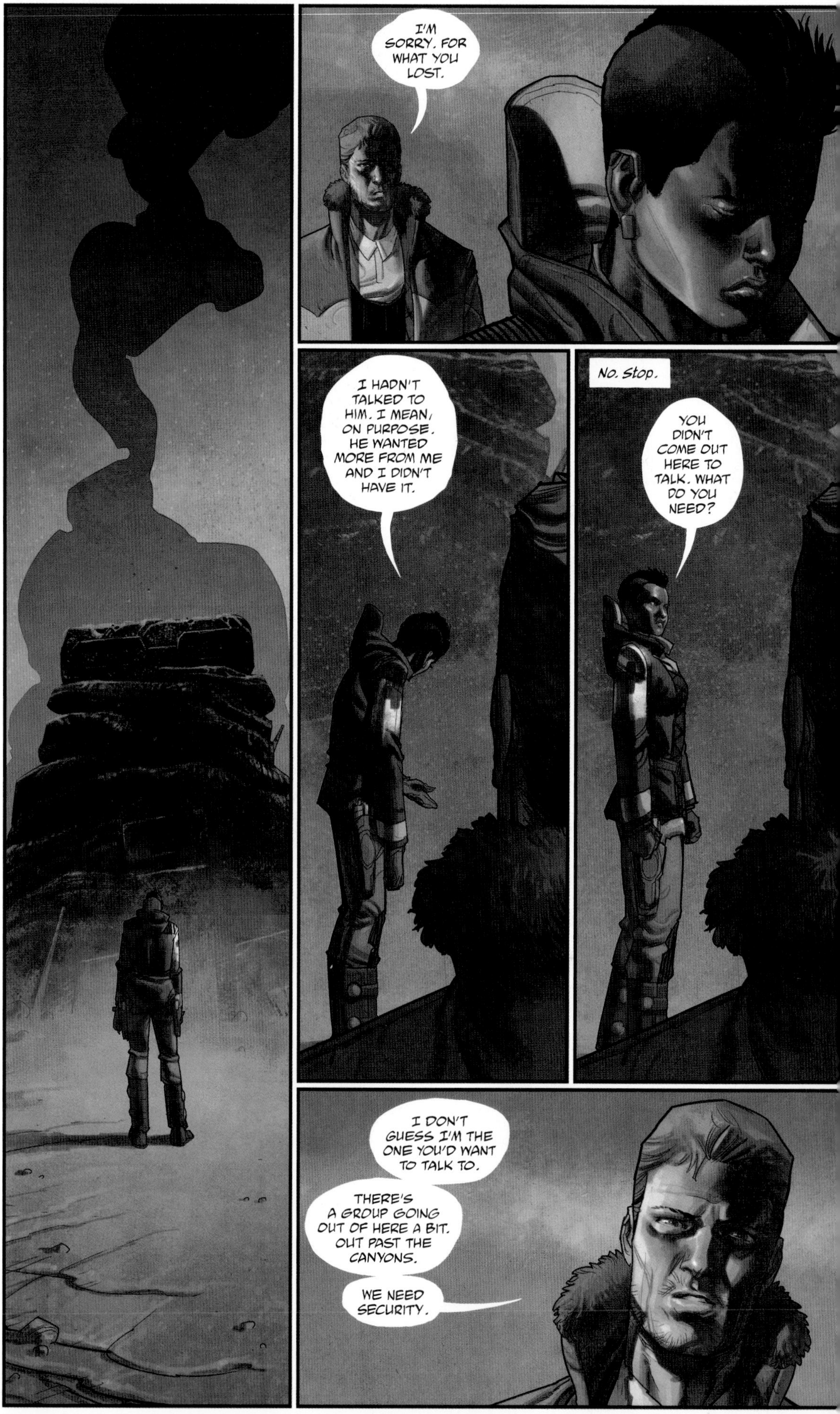
I'M SORRY. FOR WHAT YOU LOST.
I HADN'T TALKED TO HIM. I MEAN, ON PURPOSE. HE WANTED MORE FROM ME AND I DIDN'T HAVE IT.
No. Stop.
YOU DIDN'T COME OUT HERE TO TALK. WHAT DO YOU NEED?
I DON'T GUESS I'M THE ONE YOU'D WANT TO TALK TO.
THERE'S A GROUP GOING OUT OF HERE A BIT. OUT PAST THE CANYONS.
WE NEED SECURITY.

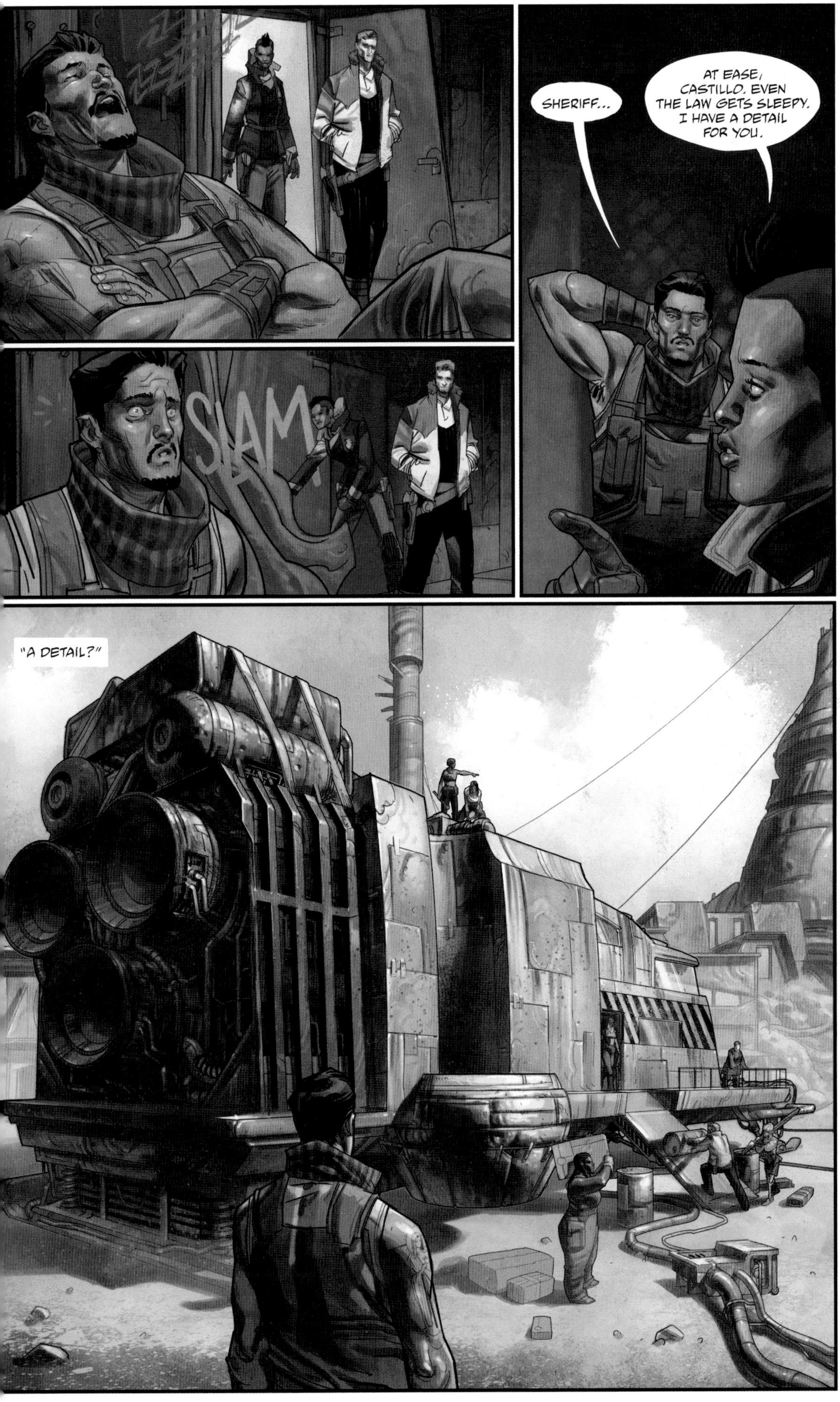
SLAM
SHERIFF...
AT EASE, CASTILLO. EVEN THE LAW GETS SLEEPY. I HAVE A DETAIL FOR YOU.
"A DETAIL?"

SHE GRINDS THE GEARS JUST THE ONCE. LEANS IN AND RIDES US PAST THE SUNS.

PAST WHAT'S FAMILIAR.

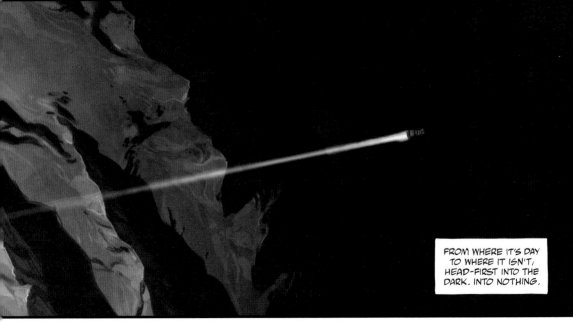

FROM WHERE IT'S DAY TO WHERE IT ISN'T, HEAD-FIRST INTO THE DARK. INTO NOTHING.

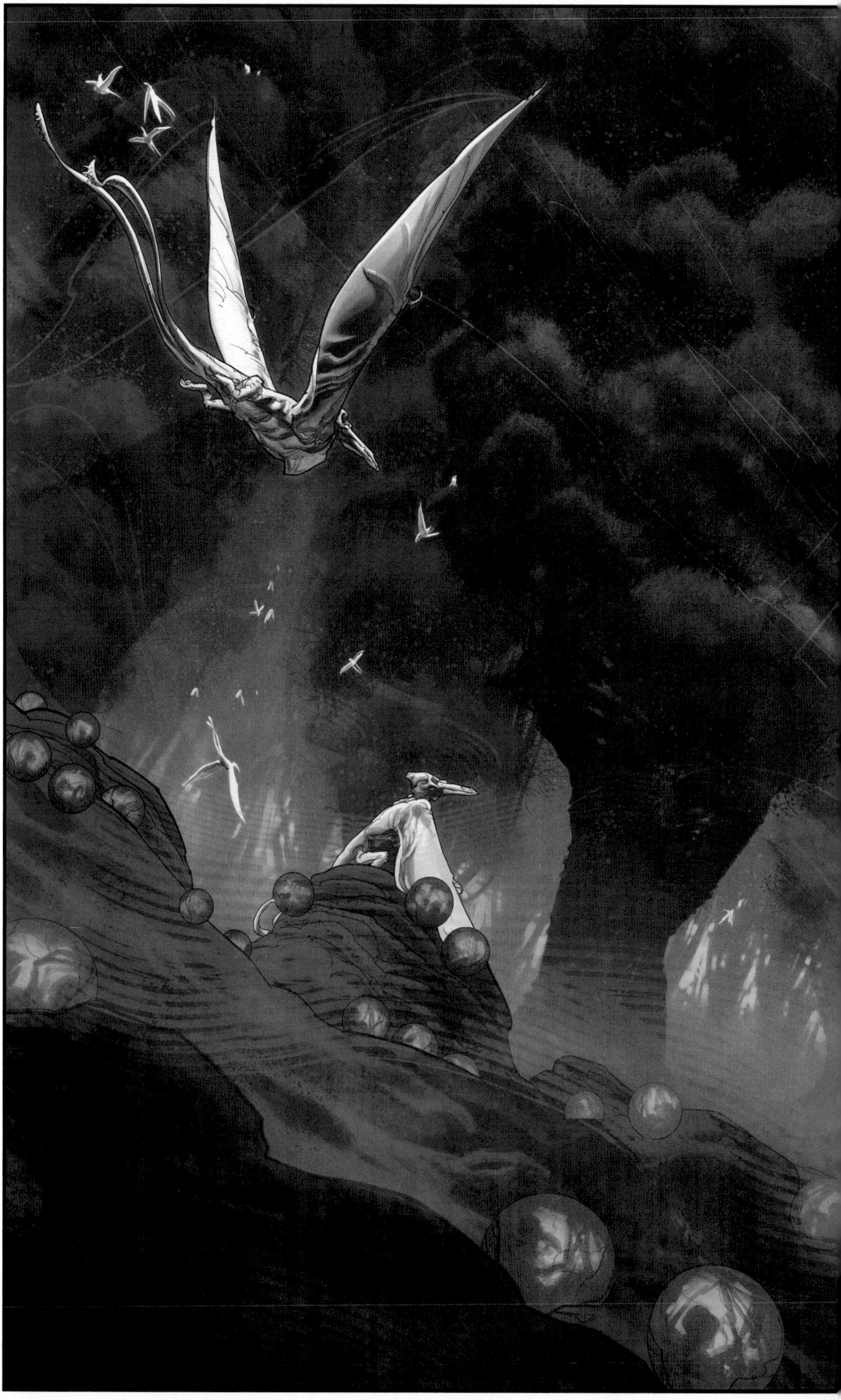

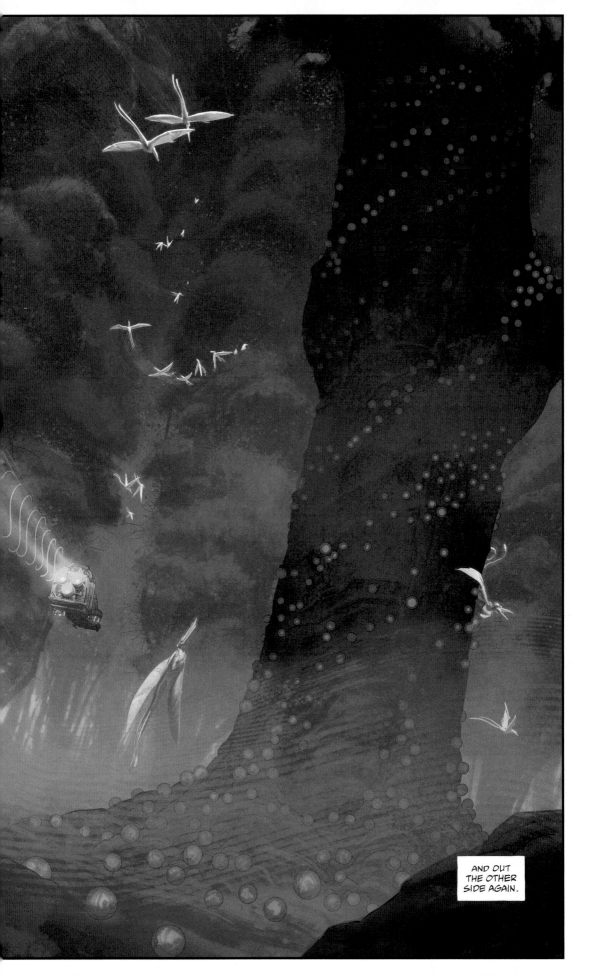

AND OUT
THE OTHER
SIDE AGAIN.

CHAPTER 7
A ROTTEN SOUND

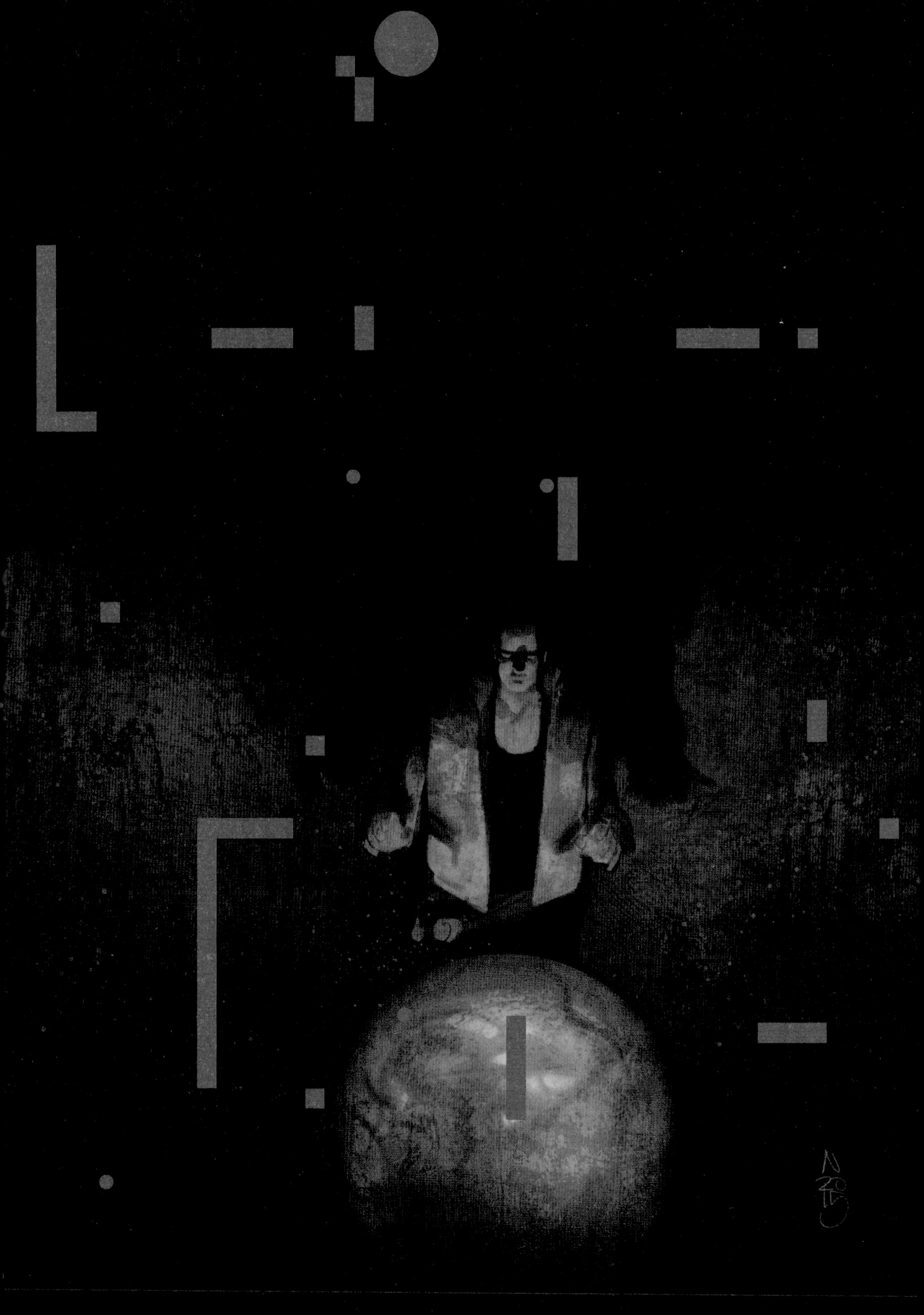

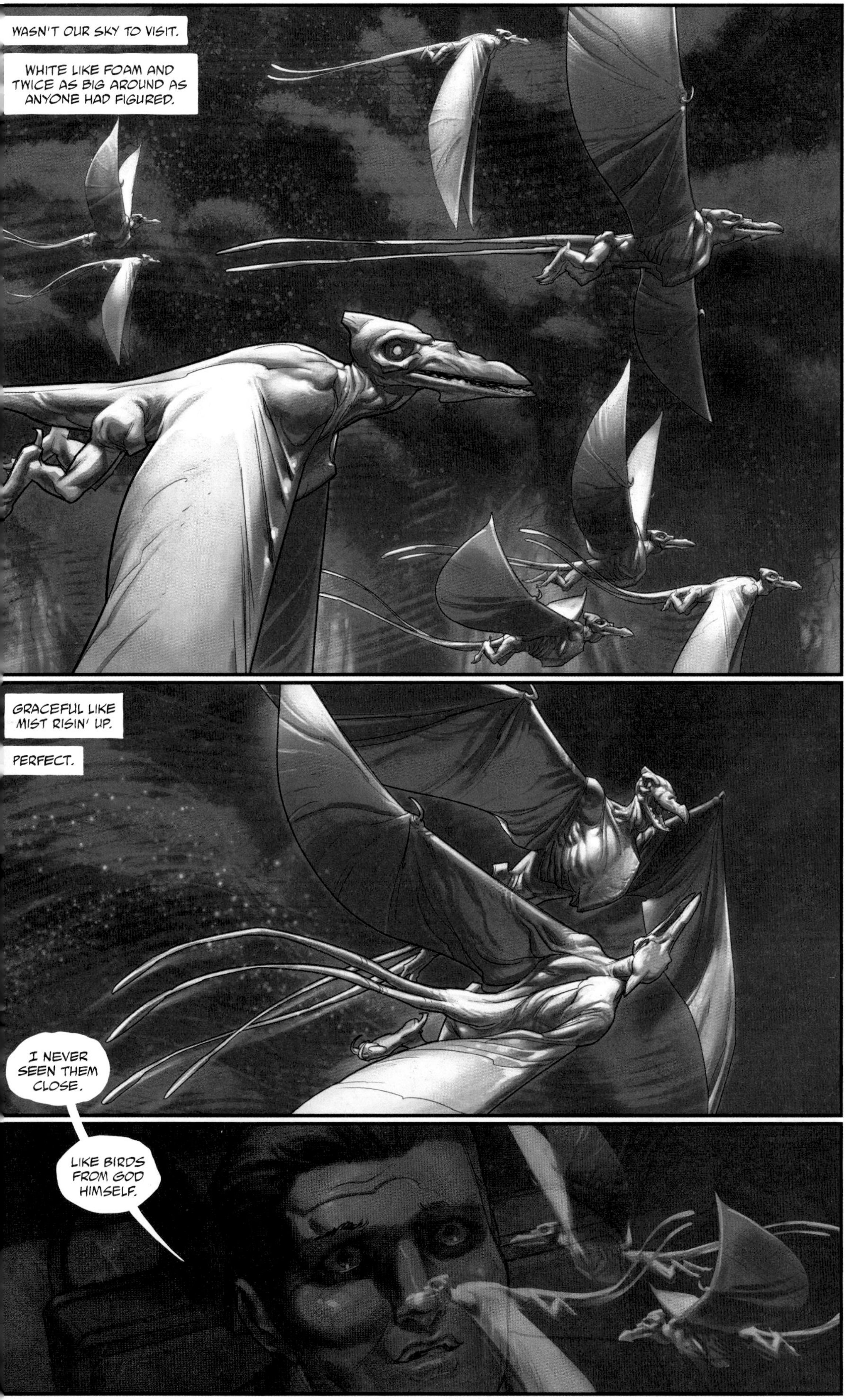
WASN'T OUR SKY TO VISIT.
WHITE LIKE FOAM AND TWICE AS BIG AROUND AS ANYONE HAD FIGURED.
GRACEFUL LIKE MIST RISIN' UP.
PERFECT.
I NEVER SEEN THEM CLOSE.
LIKE BIRDS FROM GOD HIMSELF.

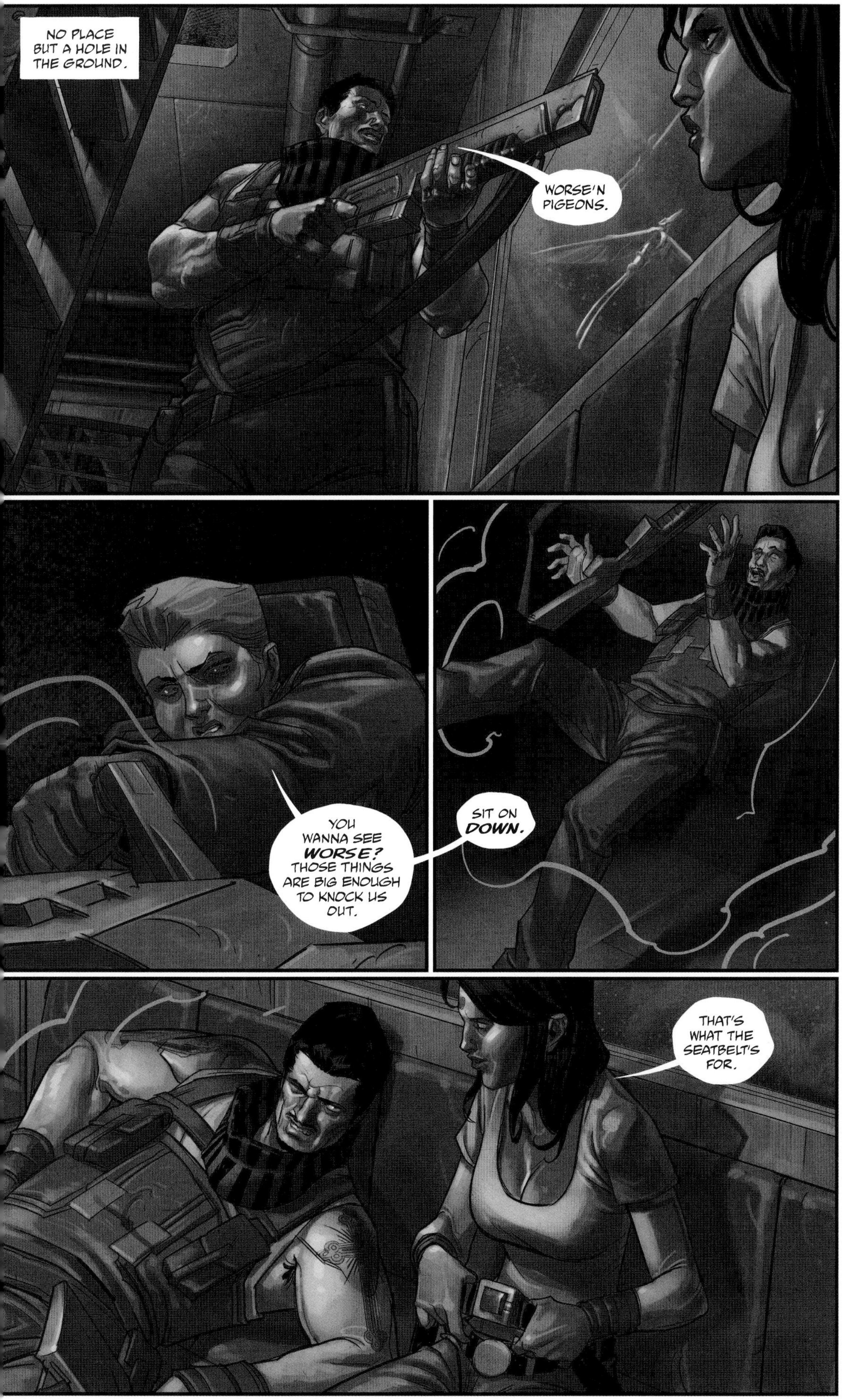
NO PLACE BUT A HOLE IN THE GROUND.
WORSE'N PIGEONS.
YOU WANNA SEE WORSE? THOSE THINGS ARE BIG ENOUGH TO KNOCK US OUT.
SIT ON DOWN.
THAT'S WHAT THE SEATBELT'S FOR.

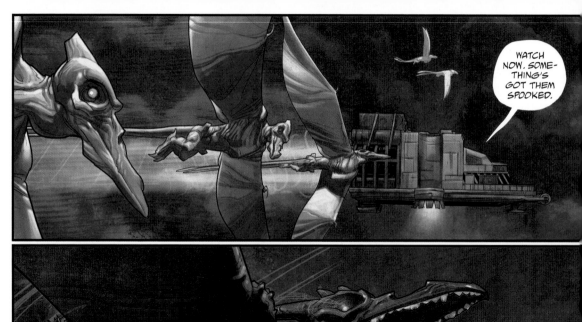

WATCH NOW. SOMETHING'S GOT THEM SPOOKED.

WORST SOUND I EVER HEARD.

A ROTTEN SOUND. A SOUND LIKE WRATH.

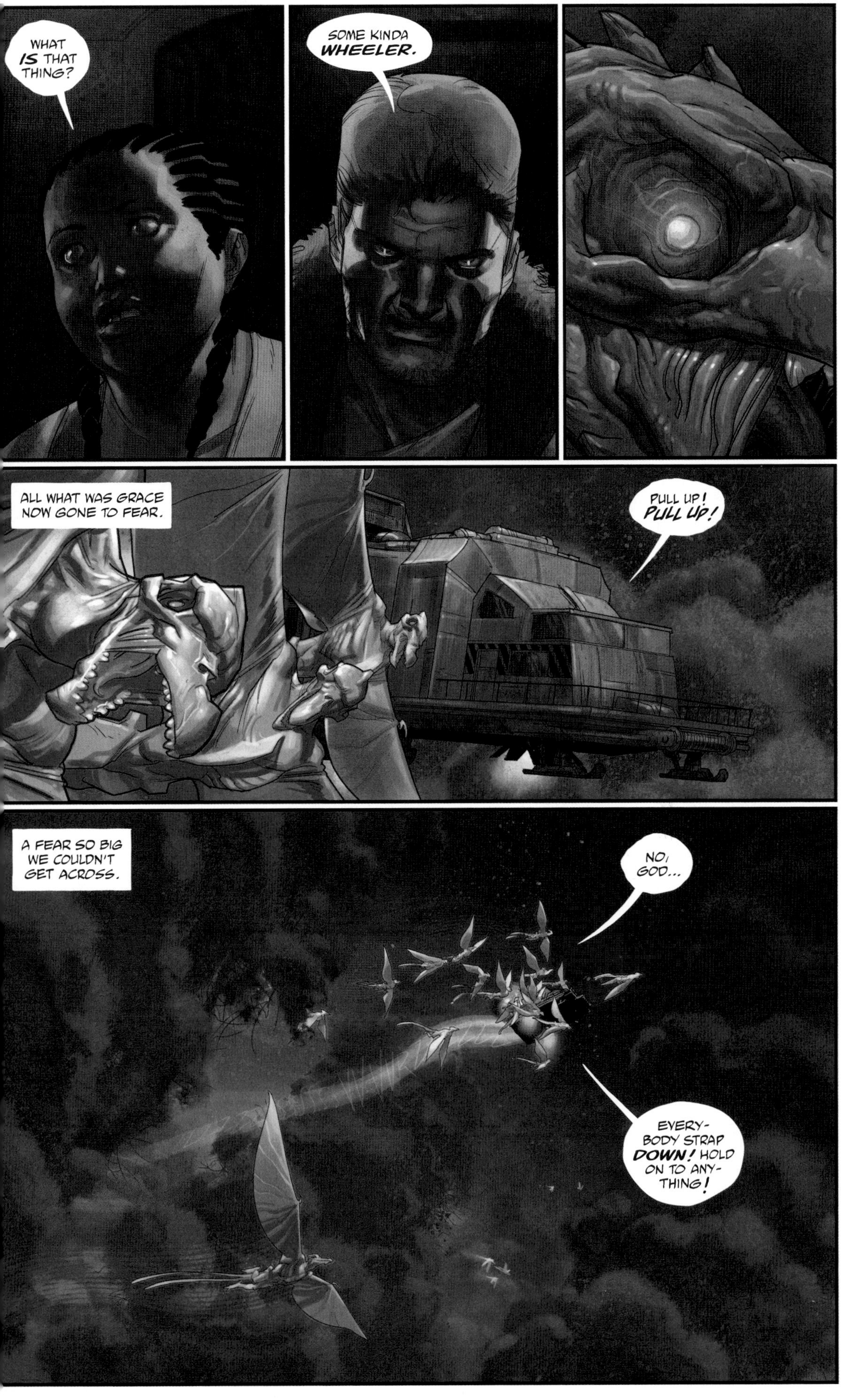
WHAT IS THAT THING?
SOME KINDA WHEELER.
ALL WHAT WAS GRACE NOW GONE TO FEAR.
PULL UP! PULL UP!
A FEAR SO BIG WE COULDN'T GET ACROSS.
NO, GOD...
EVERY-BODY STRAP DOWN! HOLD ON TO ANY-THING!

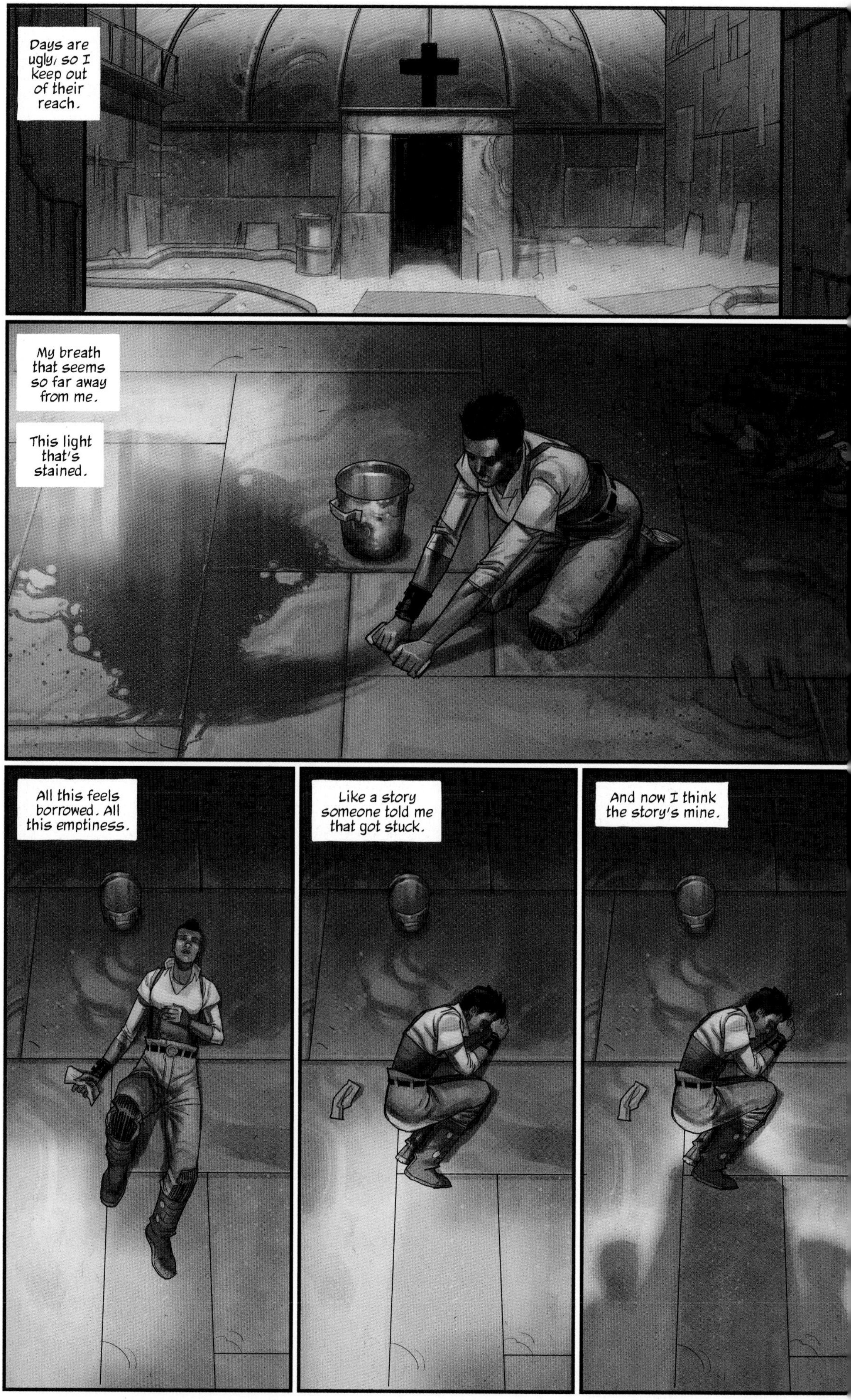
Days are ugly, so I keep out of their reach.
My breath that seems so far away from me.
This light that's stained.
All this feels borrowed. All this emptiness.
Like a story someone told me that got stuck.
And now I think the story's mine.

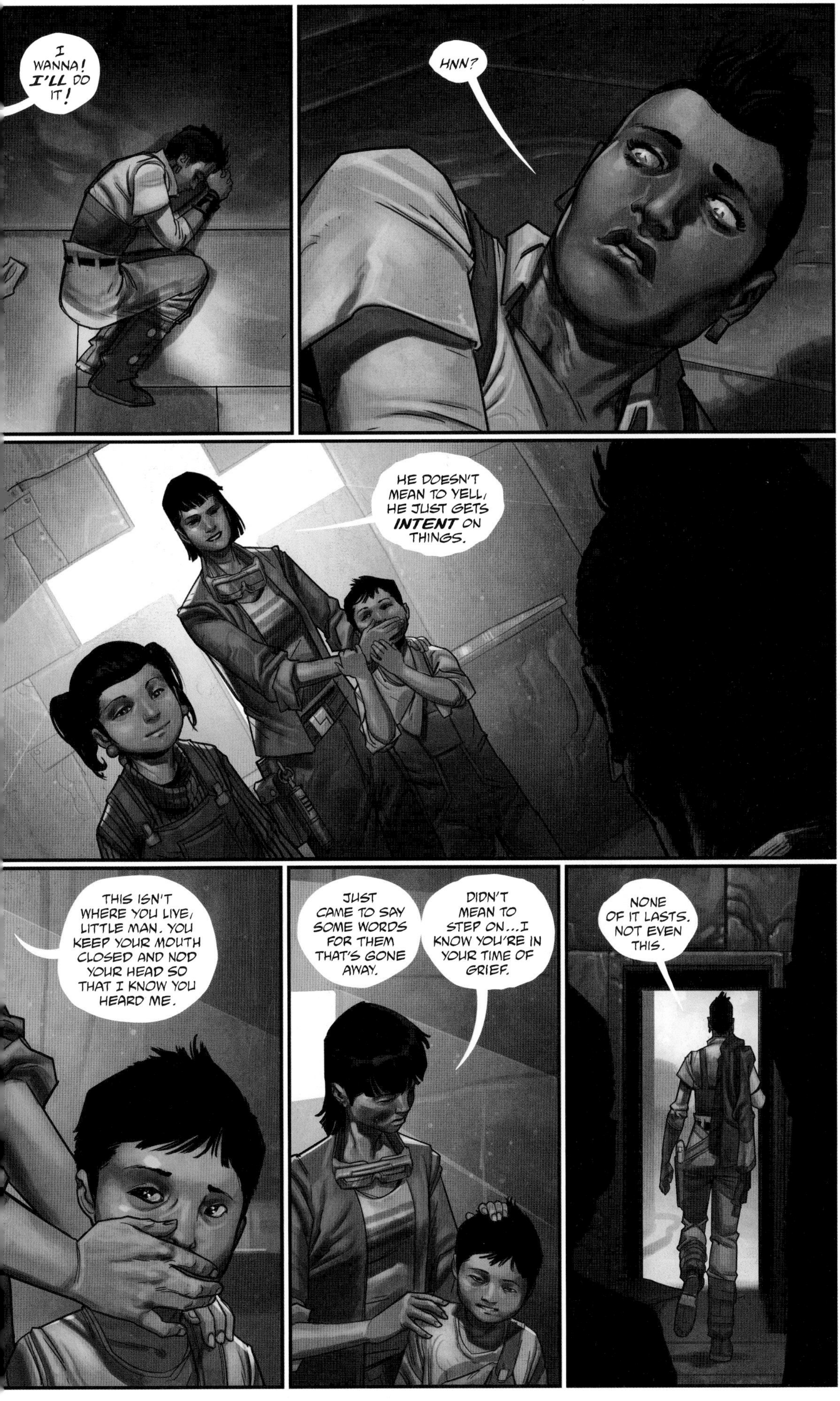
I WANNA! I'LL DO IT!
HNN?
HE DOESN'T MEAN TO YELL, HE JUST GETS INTENT ON THINGS.
THIS ISN'T WHERE YOU LIVE, LITTLE MAN. YOU KEEP YOUR MOUTH CLOSED AND NOD YOUR HEAD SO THAT I KNOW YOU HEARD ME.
JUST CAME TO SAY SOME WORDS FOR THEM THAT'S GONE AWAY.
DIDN'T MEAN TO STEP ON... I KNOW YOU'RE IN YOUR TIME OF GRIEF.
NONE OF IT LASTS. NOT EVEN THIS.

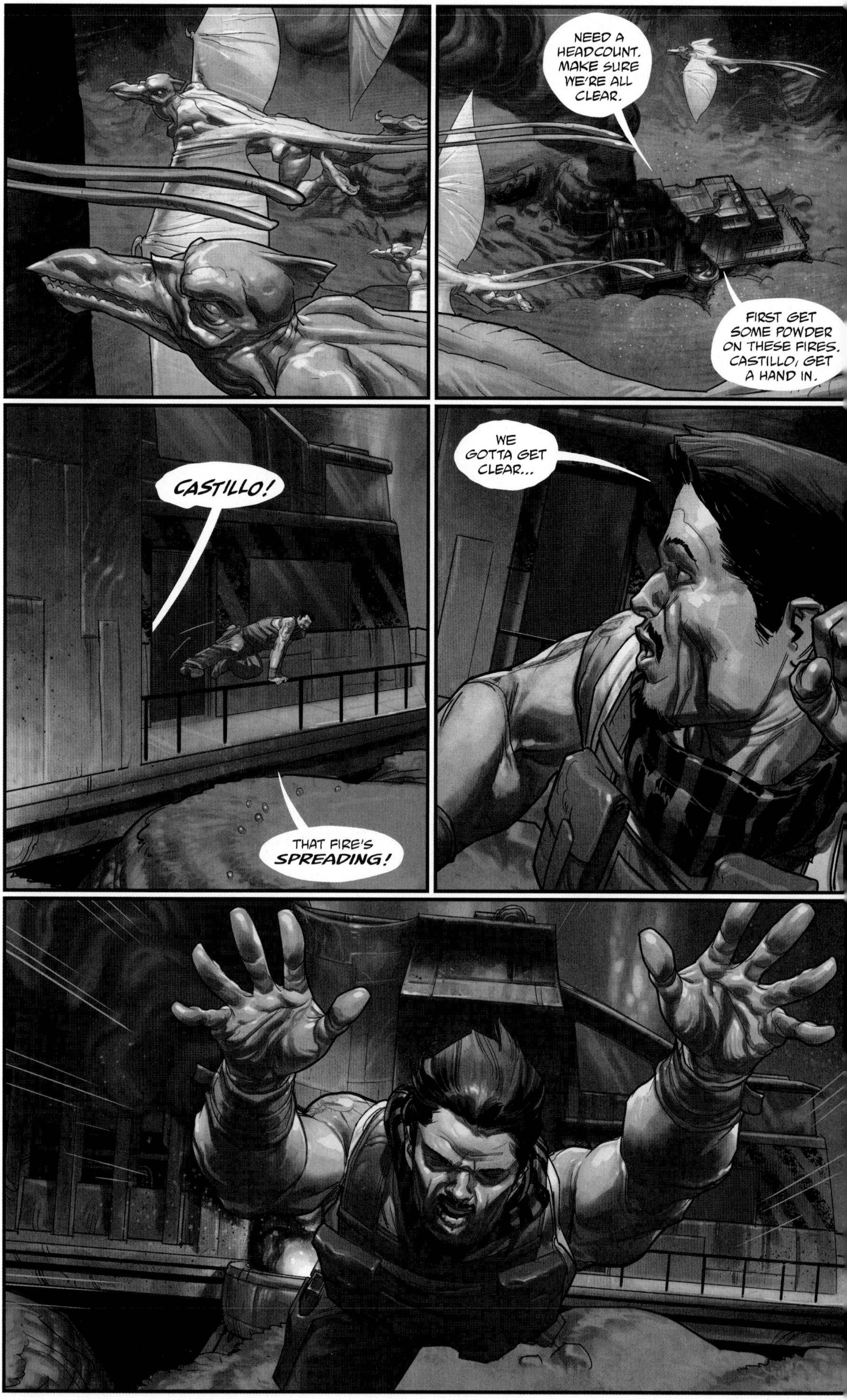
NEED A HEADCOUNT. MAKE SURE WE'RE ALL CLEAR.
FIRST GET SOME POWDER ON THESE FIRES. CASTILLO, GET A HAND IN.
CASTILLO!
THAT FIRE'S SPREADING!
WE GOTTA GET CLEAR...

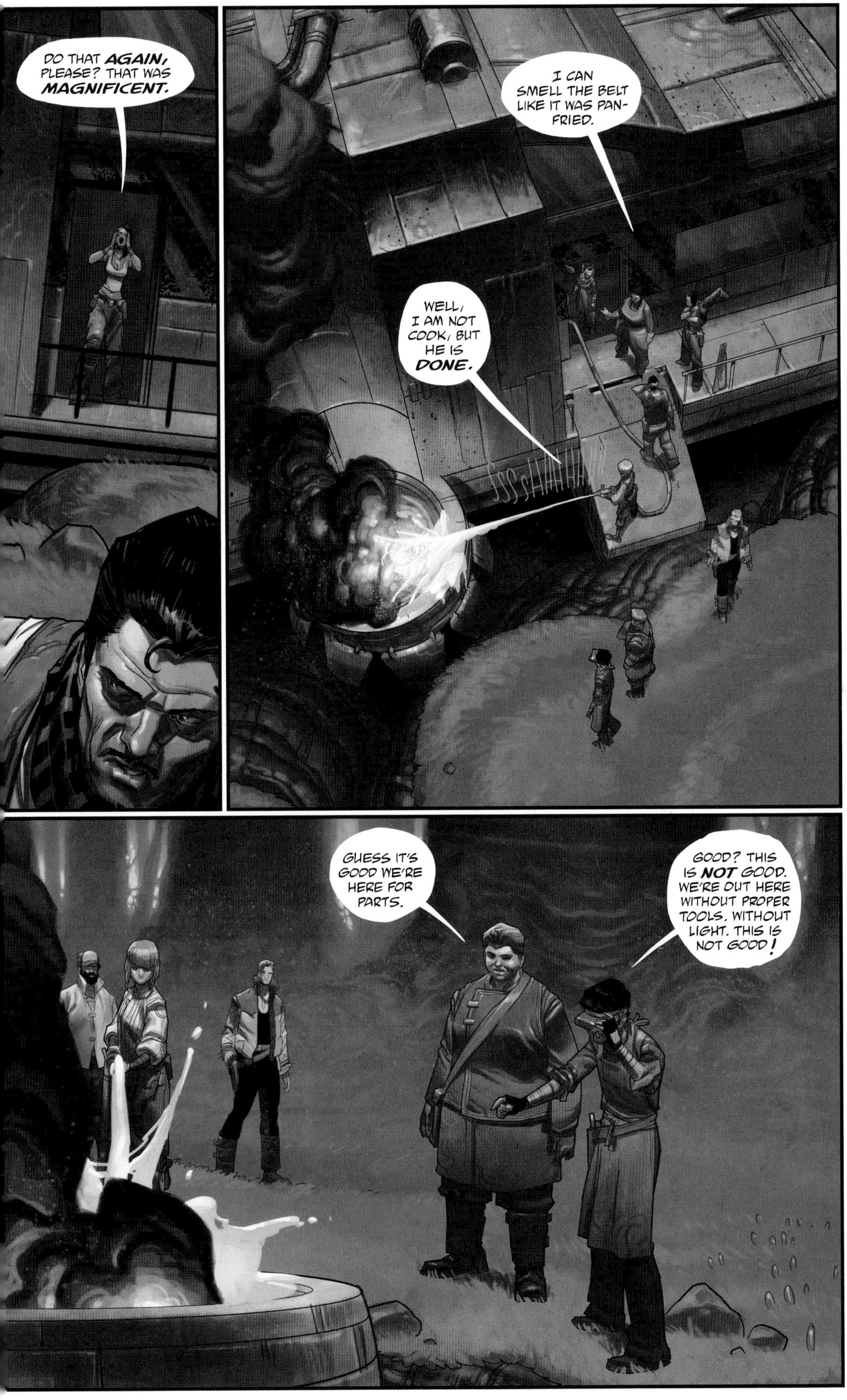
DO THAT **AGAIN,** PLEASE? THAT WAS ***MAGNIFICENT.***
I CAN SMELL THE BELT LIKE IT WAS PAN-FRIED.
WELL, I AM NOT COOK, BUT HE IS ***DONE.***
SSSSHAHHHHH
GUESS IT'S GOOD WE'RE HERE FOR PARTS.
GOOD? THIS IS ***NOT*** GOOD. WE'RE OUT HERE WITHOUT PROPER TOOLS. WITHOUT LIGHT. THIS IS NOT GOOD!

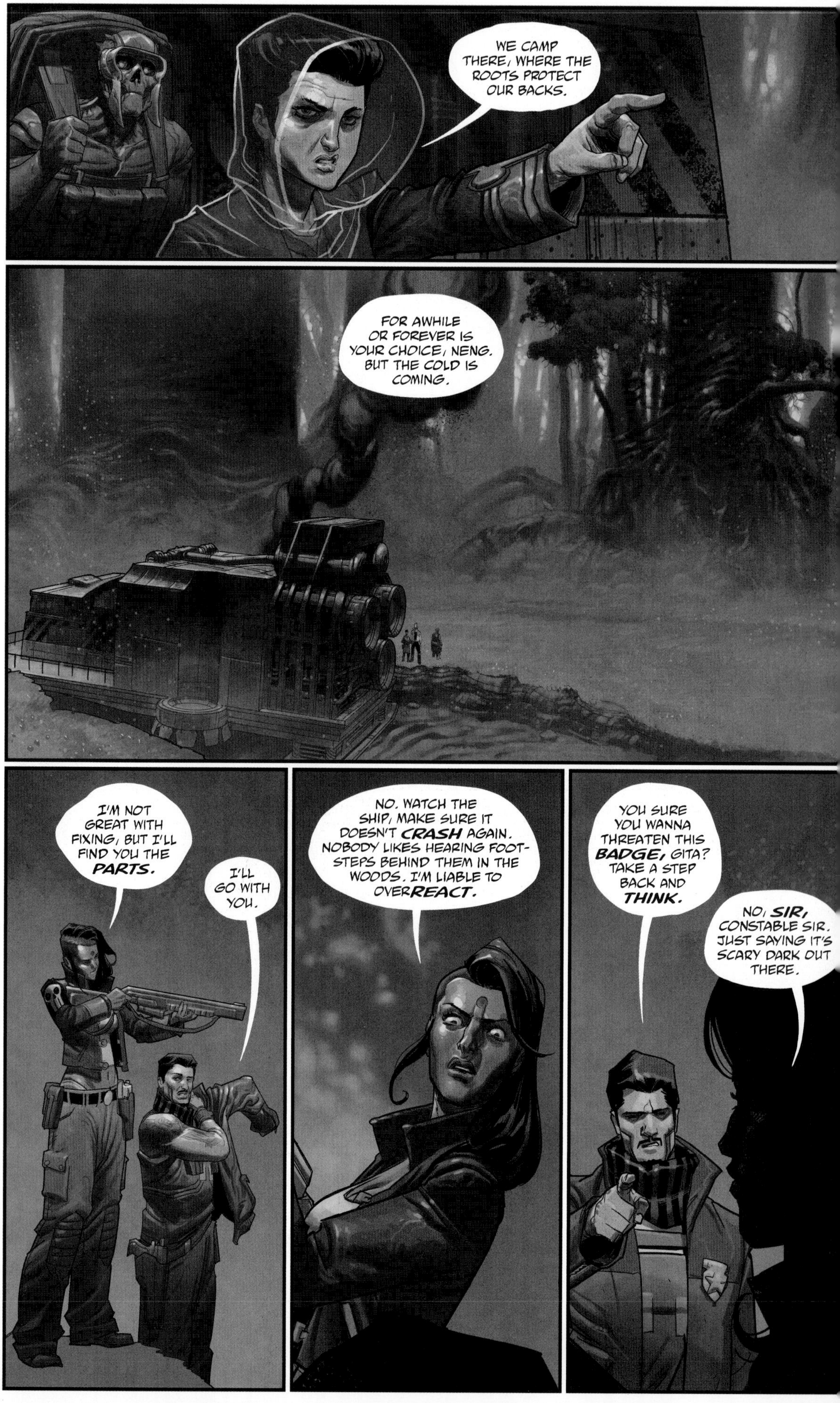
WE CAMP THERE, WHERE THE ROOTS PROTECT OUR BACKS.
FOR AWHILE OR FOREVER IS YOUR CHOICE, NENG. BUT THE COLD IS COMING.
I'M NOT GREAT WITH FIXING, BUT I'LL FIND YOU THE PARTS.
I'LL GO WITH YOU.
NO. WATCH THE SHIP, MAKE SURE IT DOESN'T CRASH AGAIN. NOBODY LIKES HEARING FOOT-STEPS BEHIND THEM IN THE WOODS. I'M LIABLE TO OVERREACT.
YOU SURE YOU WANNA THREATEN THIS BADGE, GITA? TAKE A STEP BACK AND THINK.
NO, SIR, CONSTABLE SIR. JUST SAYING IT'S SCARY DARK OUT THERE.

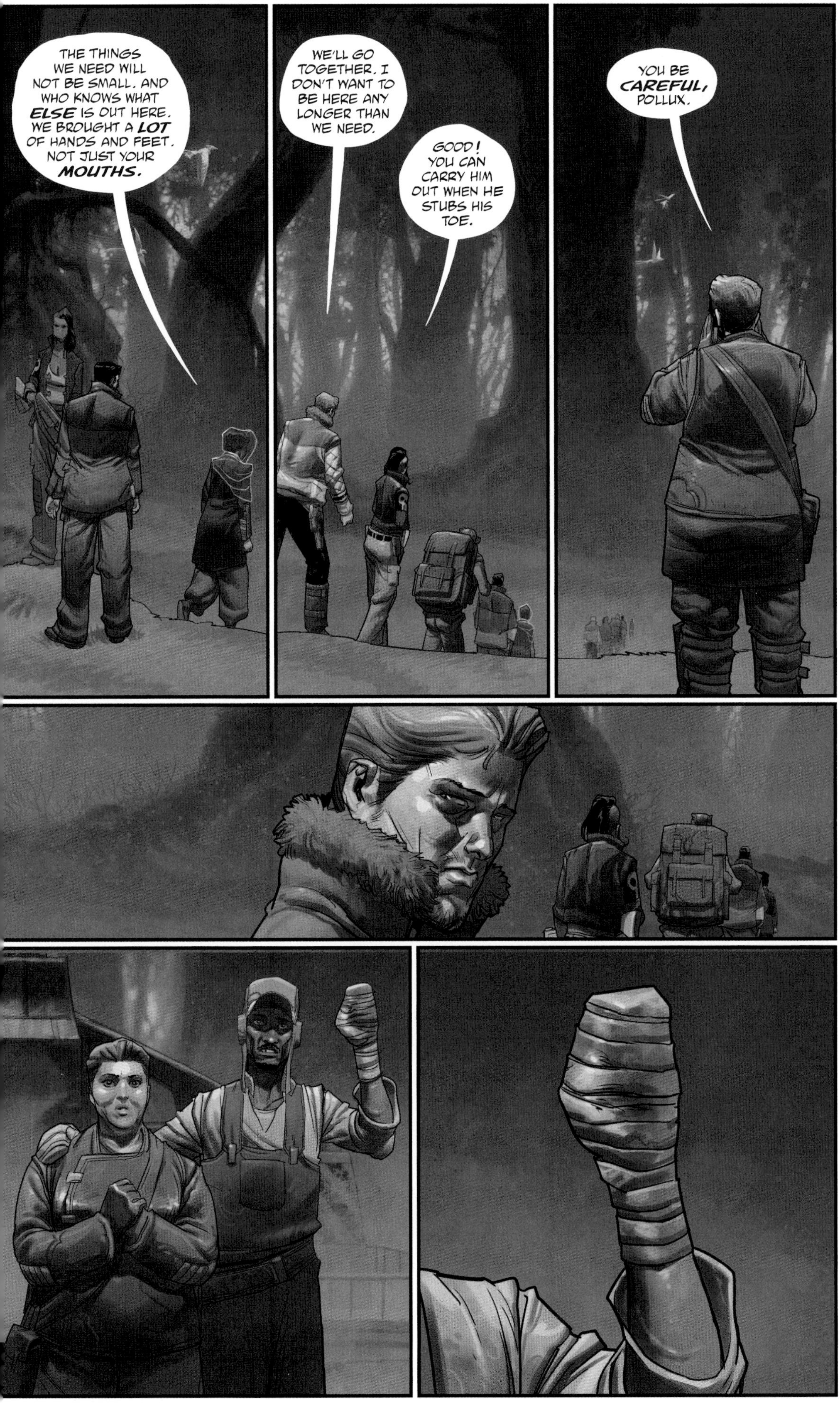
THE THINGS WE NEED WILL NOT BE SMALL. AND WHO KNOWS WHAT ELSE IS OUT HERE. WE BROUGHT A LOT OF HANDS AND FEET. NOT JUST YOUR MOUTHS.
WE'LL GO TOGETHER. I DON'T WANT TO BE HERE ANY LONGER THAN WE NEED.
GOOD! YOU CAN CARRY HIM OUT WHEN HE STUBS HIS TOE.
YOU BE CAREFUL, POLLUX.

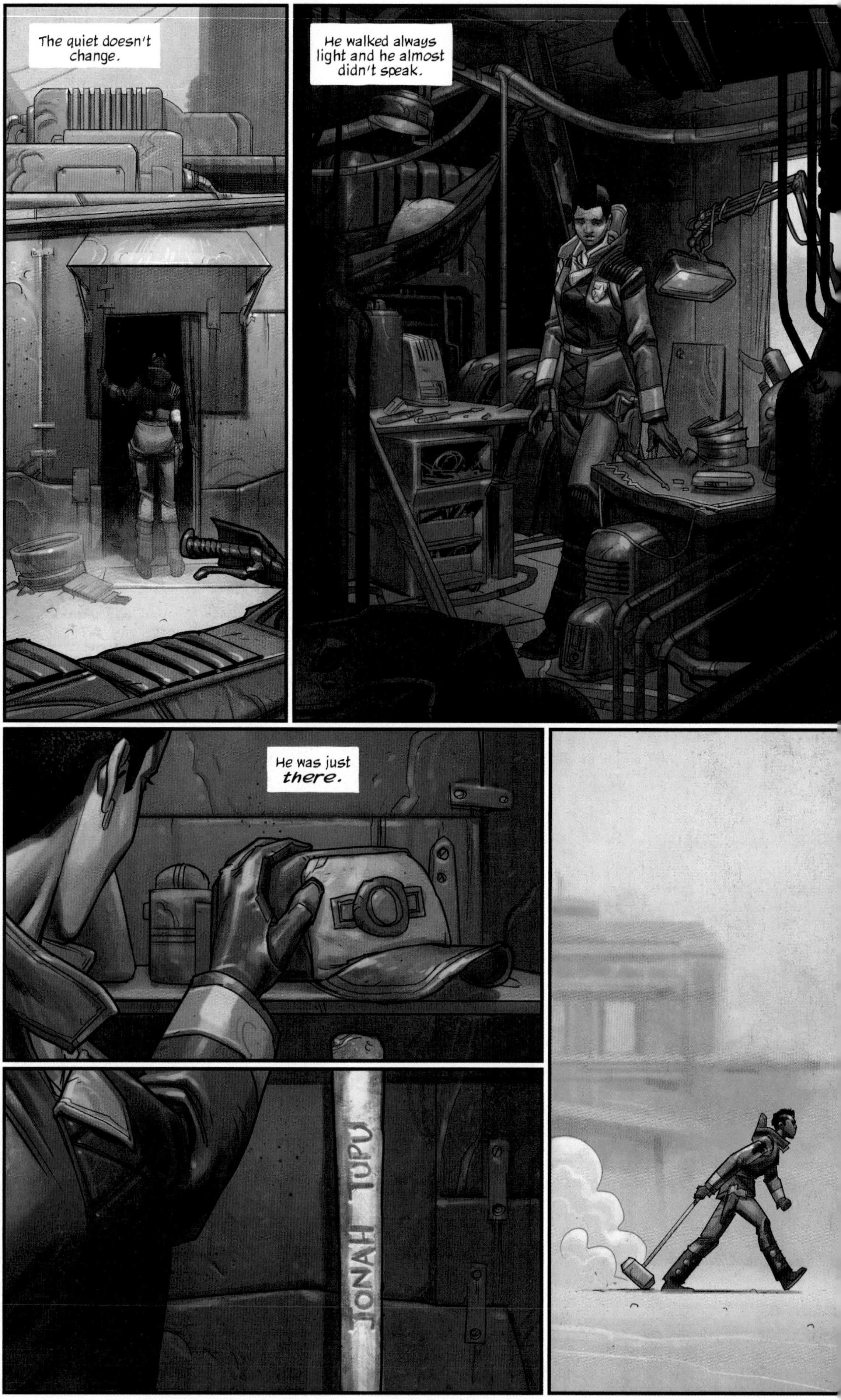

The quiet doesn't change.
He walked always light and he almost didn't speak.
He was just *there.*
JONAH TUPU

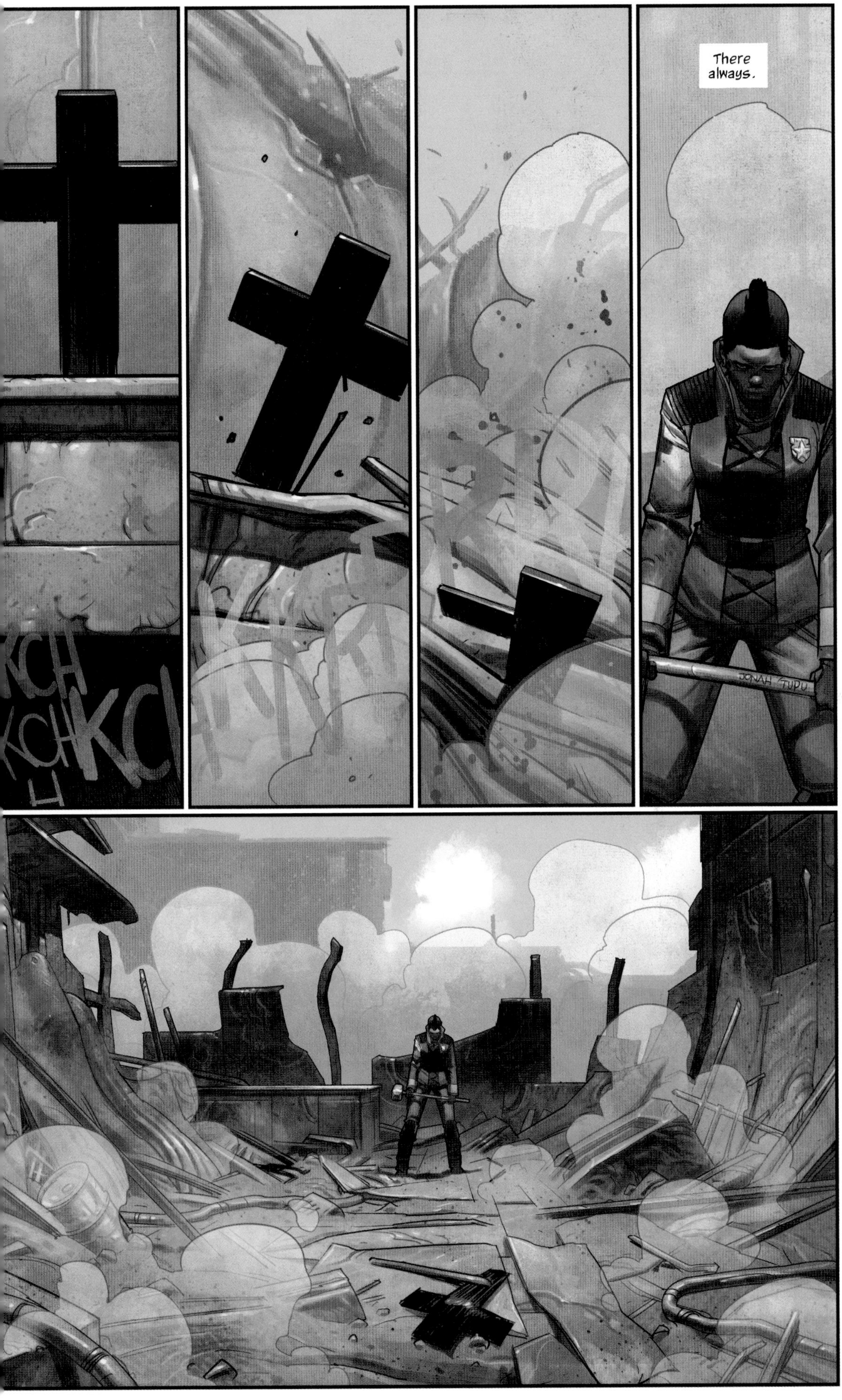

There always.
JONAH TUPU

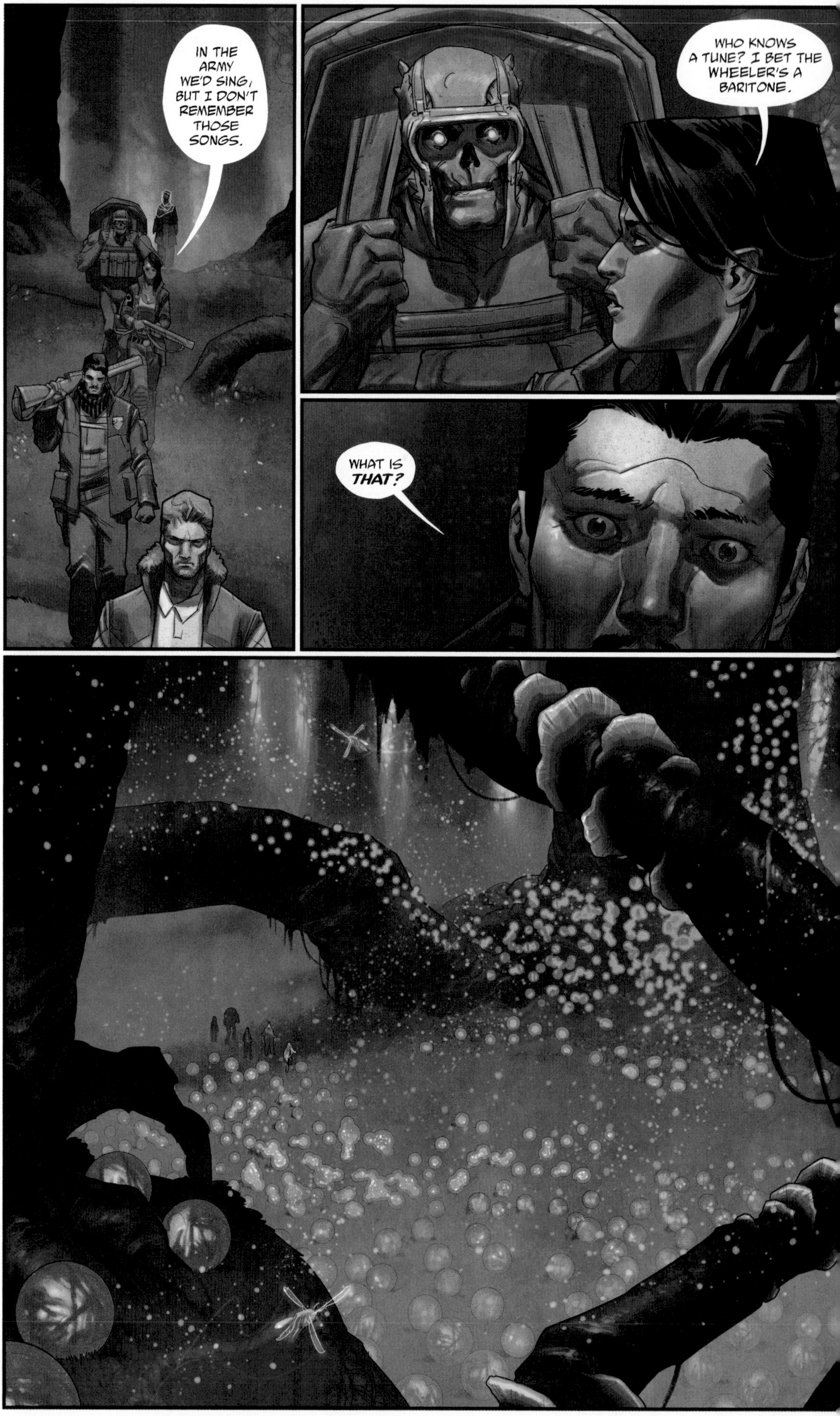
IN THE ARMY WE'D SING, BUT I DON'T REMEMBER THOSE SONGS.
WHO KNOWS A TUNE? I BET THE WHEELER'S A BARITONE.
WHAT IS *THAT?*

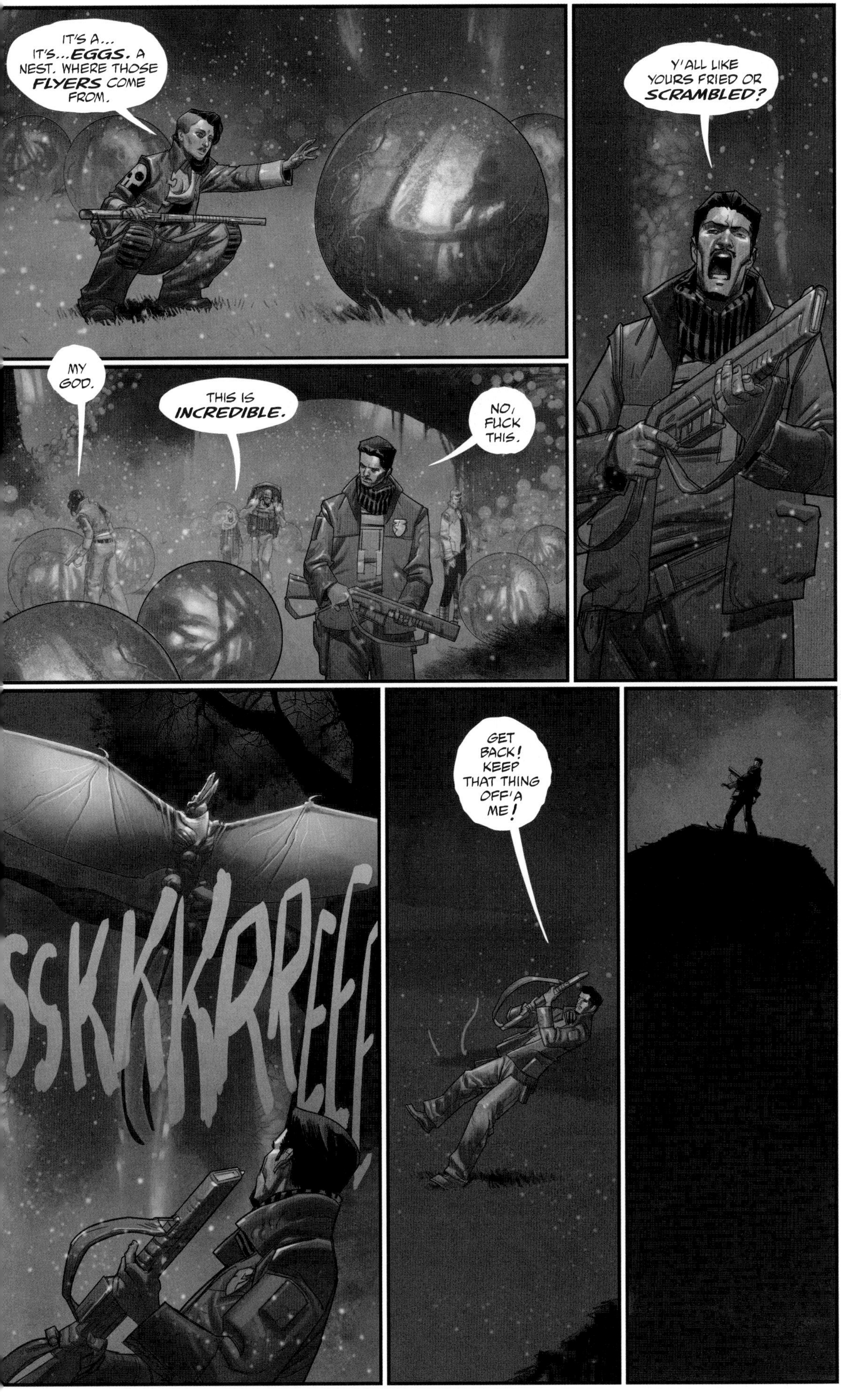
IT'S A... IT'S...EGGS. A NEST. WHERE THOSE FLYERS COME FROM.
Y'ALL LIKE YOURS FRIED OR SCRAMBLED?
MY GOD.
THIS IS INCREDIBLE.
NO, FUCK THIS.
SSKKKREEE
GET BACK! KEEP THAT THING OFF'A ME!

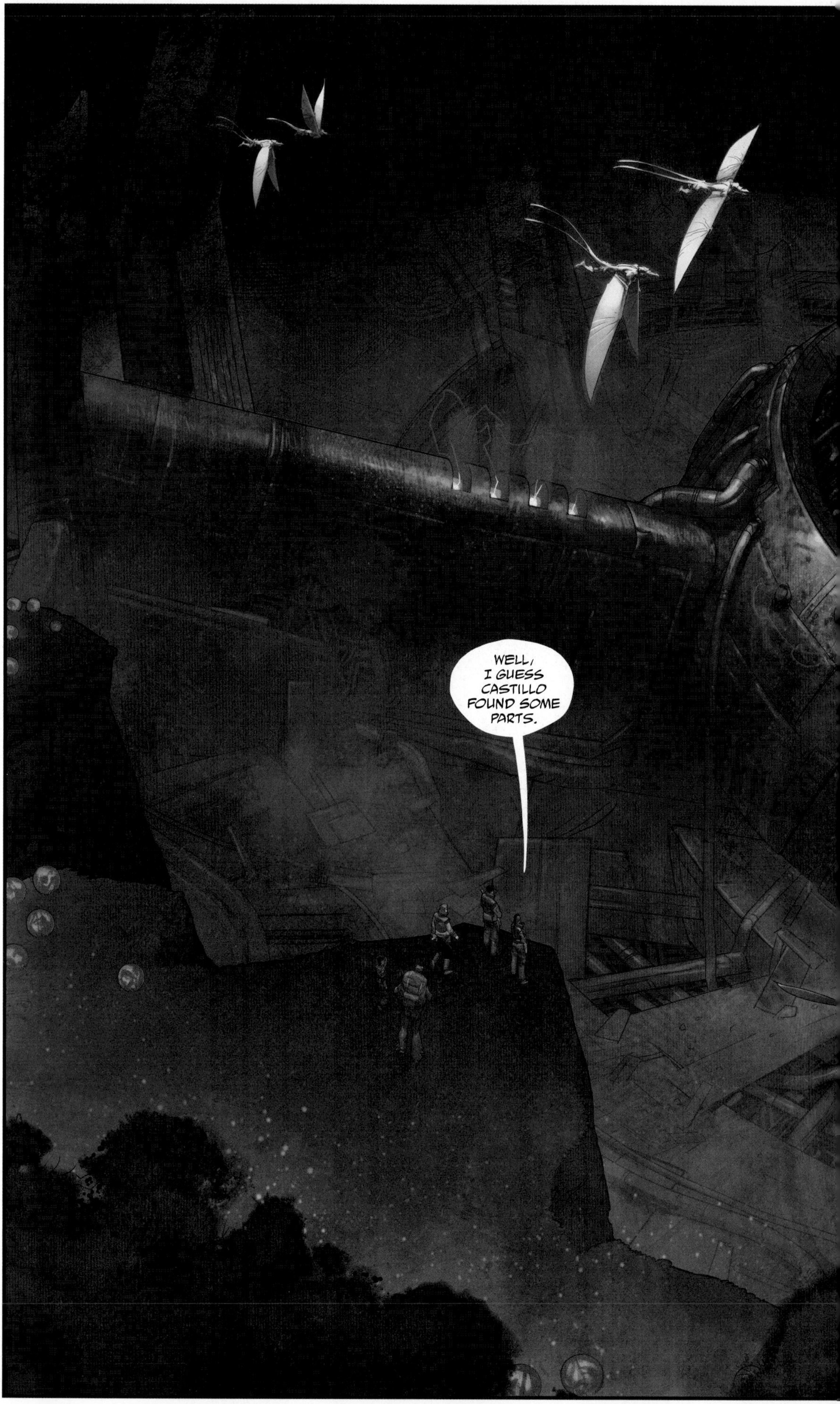
WELL, I GUESS CASTILLO FOUND SOME PARTS.

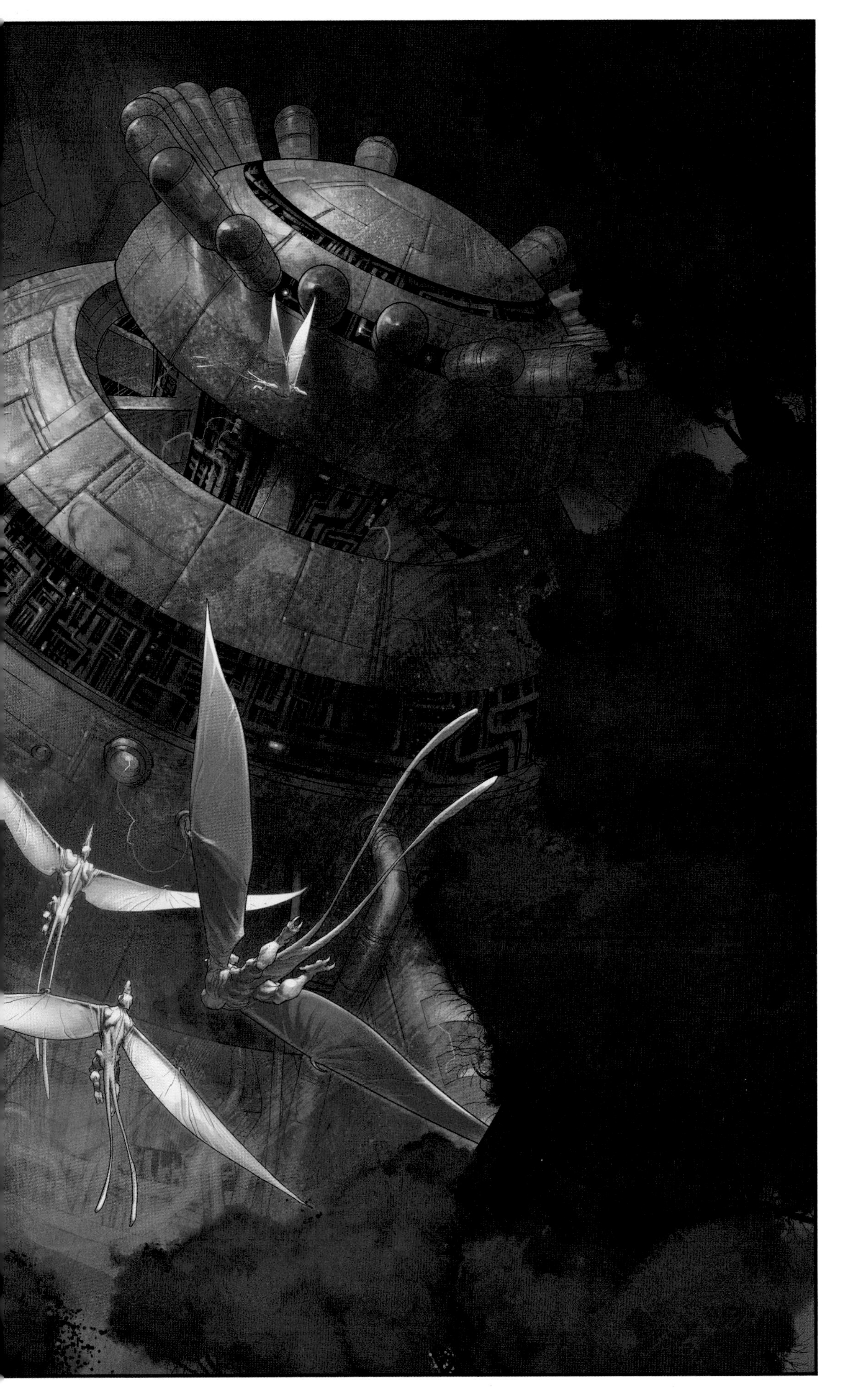

Can't mend what's lost.

How do you get right with the dead?

JONAH...

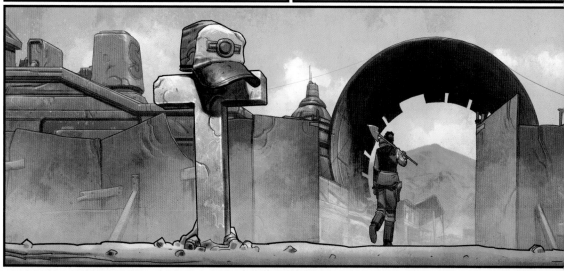

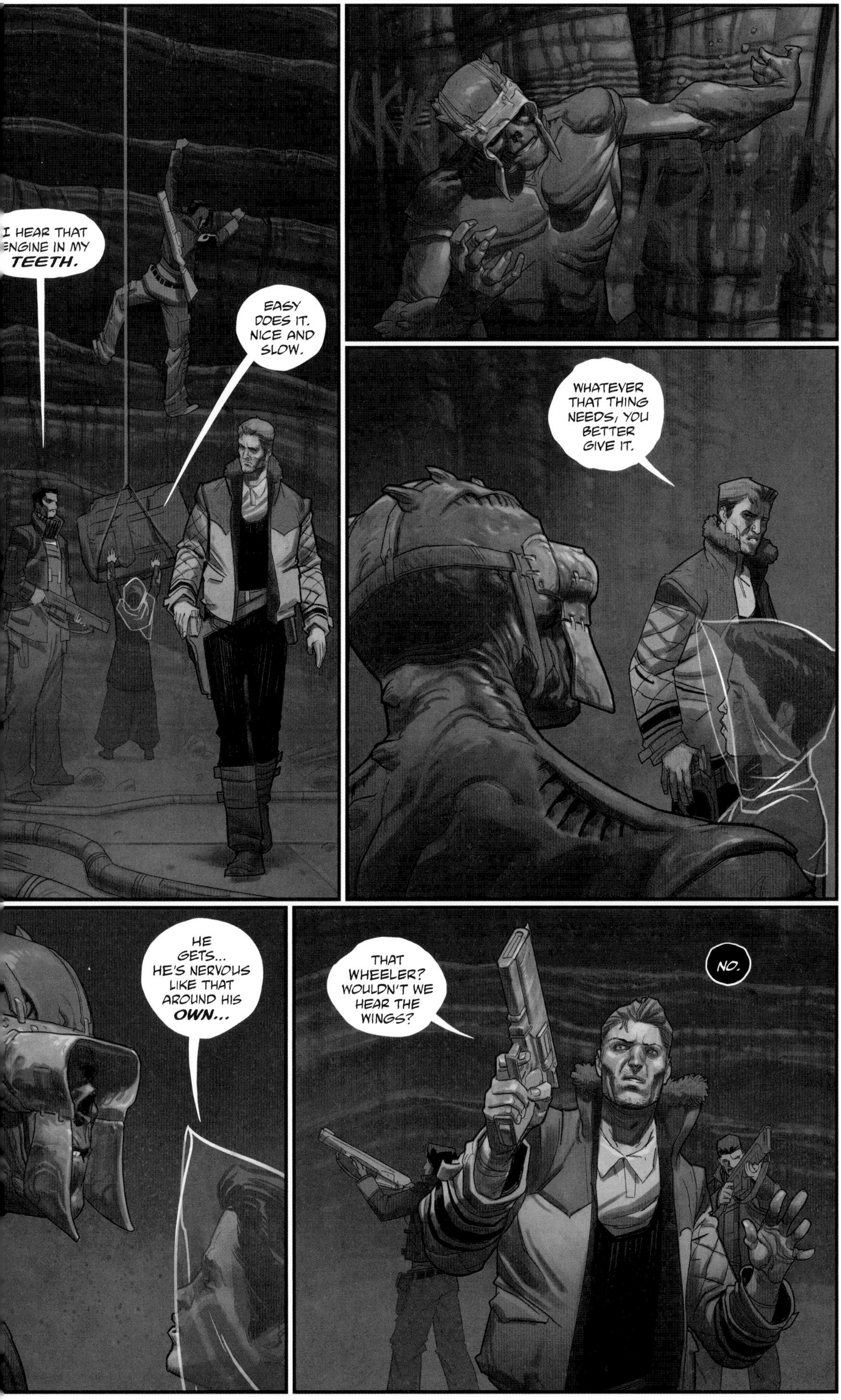
I HEAR THAT ENGINE IN MY TEETH.
EASY DOES IT. NICE AND SLOW.
WHATEVER THAT THING NEEDS, YOU BETTER GIVE IT.
HE GETS... HE'S NERVOUS LIKE THAT AROUND HIS OWN...
THAT WHEELER? WOULDN'T WE HEAR THE WINGS?
NO.

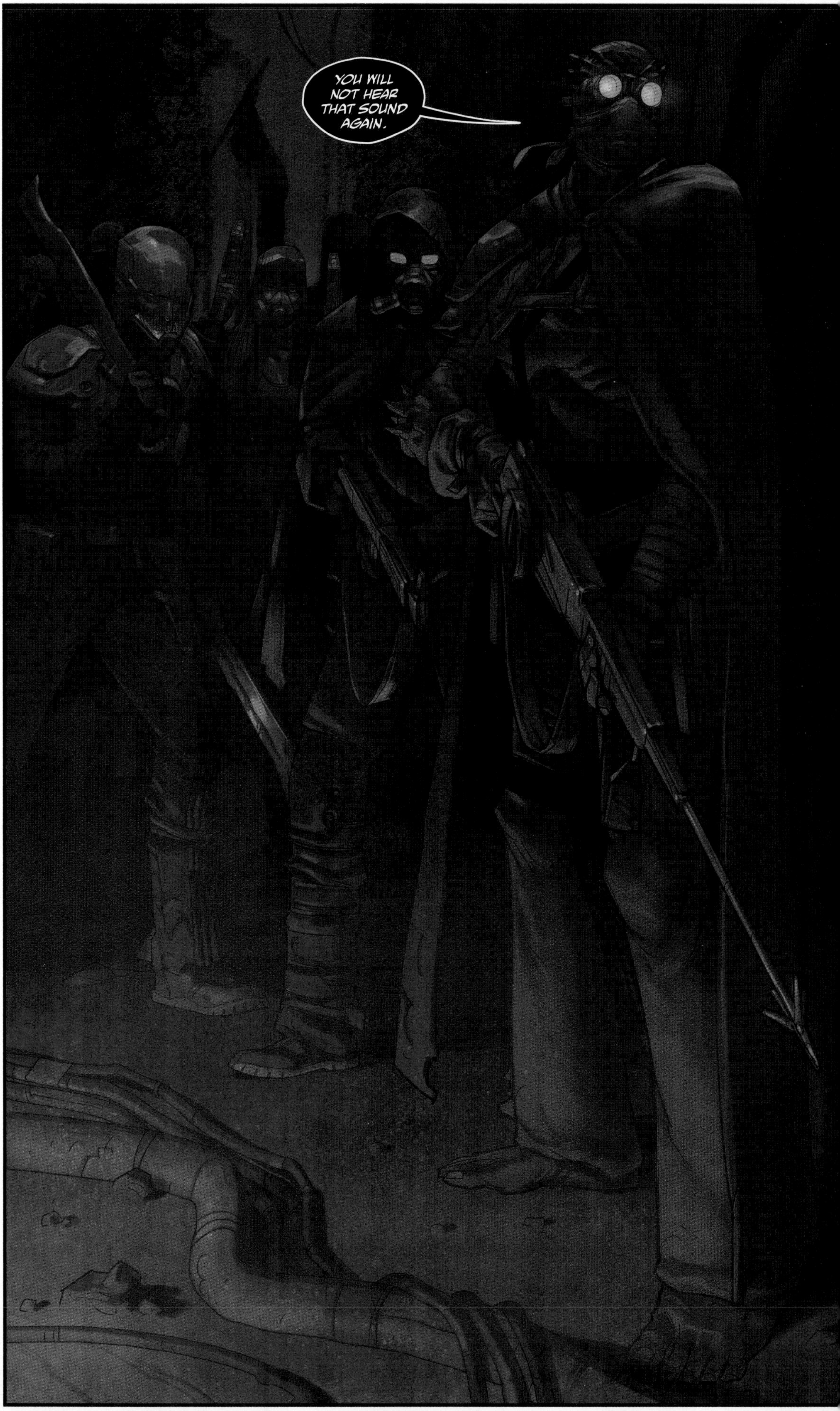
YOU WILL NOT HEAR THAT SOUND AGAIN.

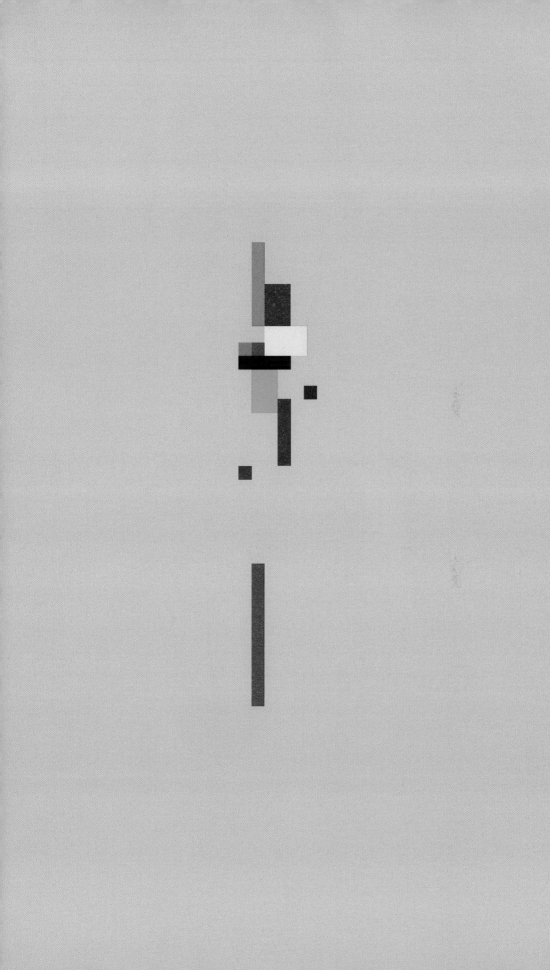

CHAPTER 8
FITTING IN

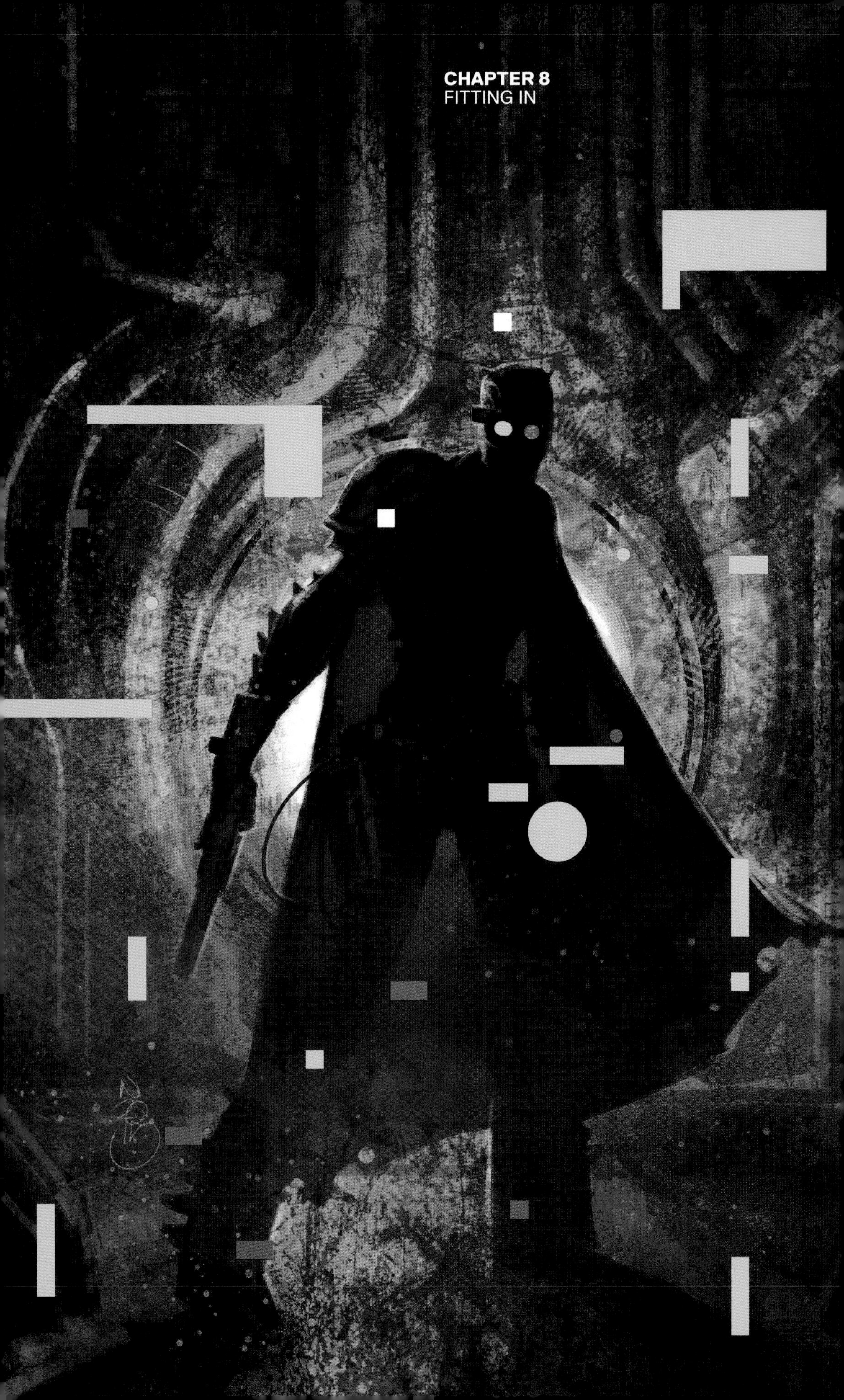

WE NEED TO STAND UP HERE AND SMACK 'EM DOWN.

YOU DIDN'T HEAR THAT VOICE? THAT WAS A WHEELER *BOSS*. *THEY* DO THE SMACKING.

I KNOW THE SONG.

THE SOUNDS OF VIOLENCE OVERHEAD LIKE WIND.

MADNESS AND DREAD THAT TANGLE UP UNTIL THEY'RE BOTH ONE THING.

FEELS LIKE THE FIRST TIME I BELONG HERE.

YOU WANNA CRAWL DOWN IN A HOLE LIKE *RATS*?

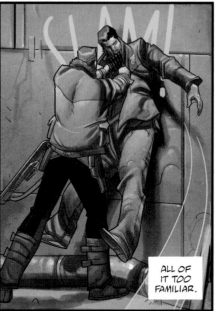

ALL OF IT TOO FAMILIAR.

THINK YOU KNOW WHO I AM?

ALL MY ANGER FINALLY FINDS AN EASY PLACE.

TOO EASY, MAYBE.

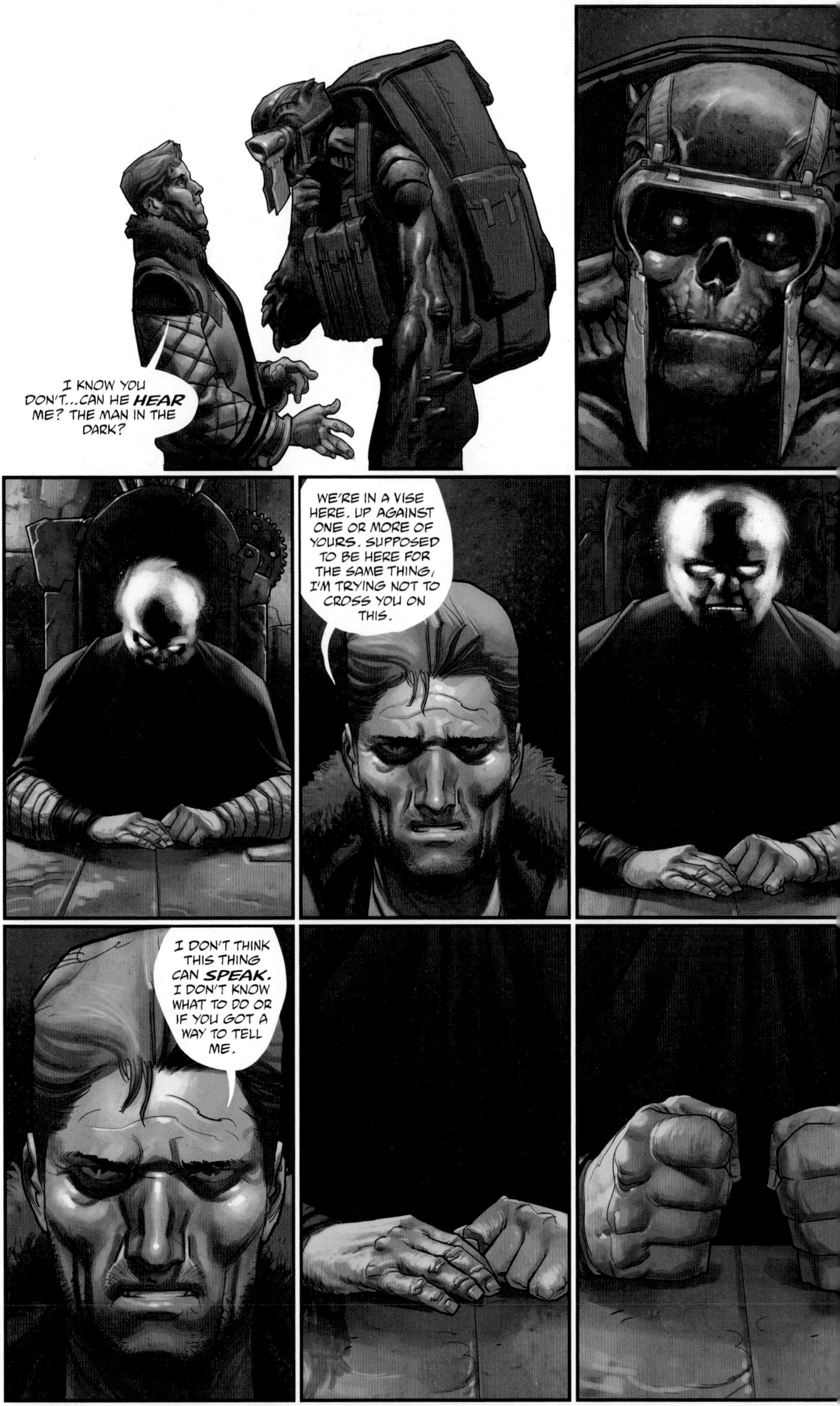
I KNOW YOU DON'T...CAN HE HEAR ME? THE MAN IN THE DARK?
WE'RE IN A VISE HERE. UP AGAINST ONE OR MORE OF YOURS. SUPPOSED TO BE HERE FOR THE SAME THING, I'M TRYING NOT TO CROSS YOU ON THIS.
I DON'T THINK THIS THING CAN SPEAK. I DON'T KNOW WHAT TO DO OR IF YOU GOT A WAY TO TELL ME.

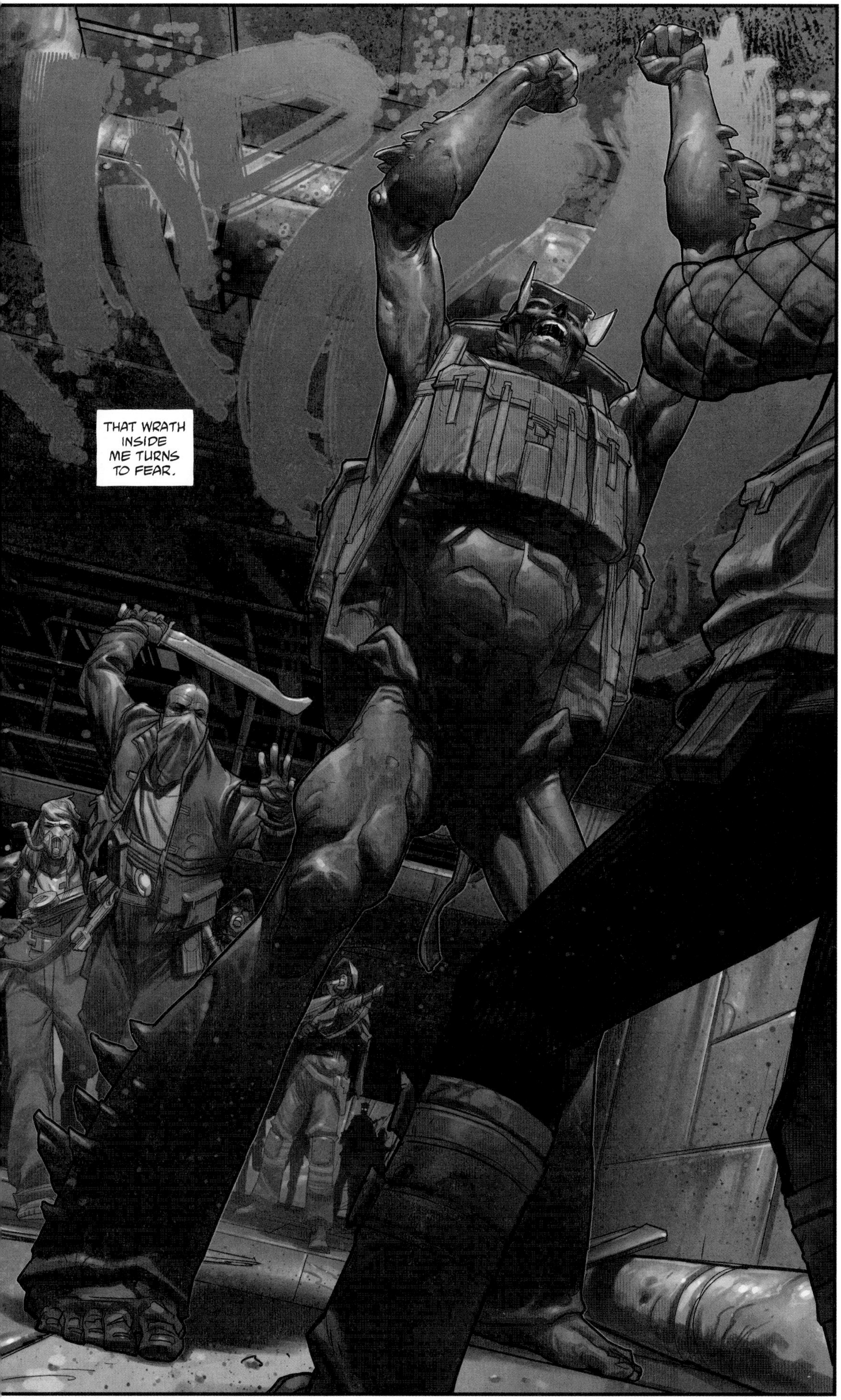
THAT WRATH INSIDE ME TURNS TO FEAR.

THE FIRE WASHED OUT BY SOMETHING BIGGER.

SO BIG I THINK IT'S GOING TO TAKE US ALL.

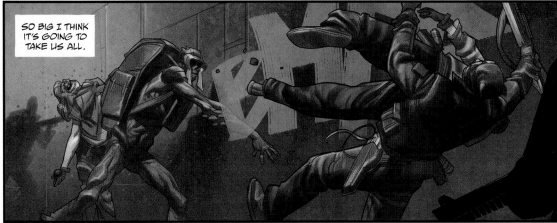

MADRE DE CRISTO.

ENJOY THE SHOW, CONSTABLE. *I'LL* GET THIS.

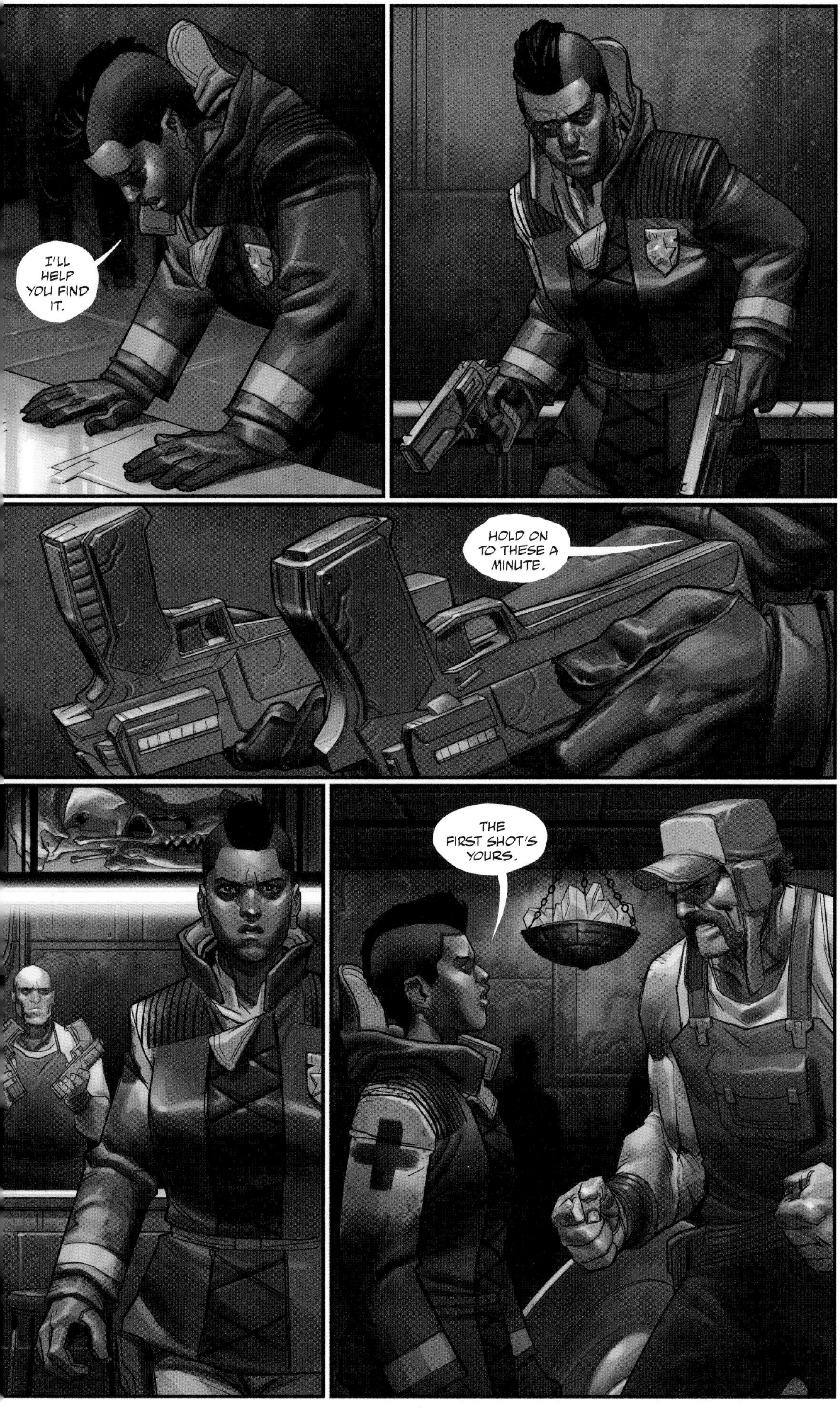
I'LL HELP YOU FIND IT.
HOLD ON TO THESE A MINUTE.
THE FIRST SHOT'S YOURS.

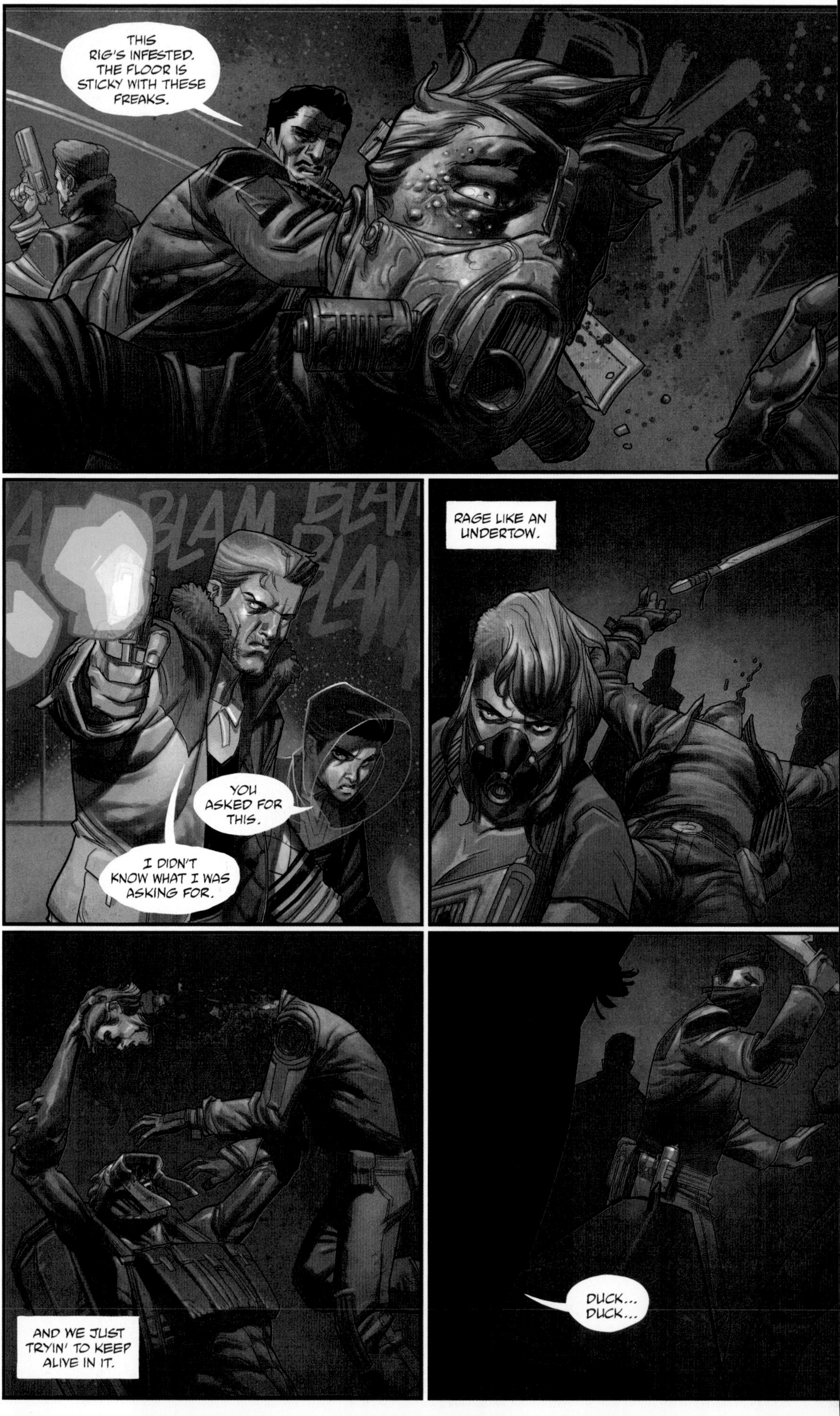
THIS RIG'S INFESTED. THE FLOOR IS STICKY WITH THESE FREAKS.
BLAM
YOU ASKED FOR THIS.
I DIDN'T KNOW WHAT I WAS ASKING FOR.
RAGE LIKE AN UNDERTOW.
AND WE JUST TRYIN' TO KEEP ALIVE IN IT.
DUCK... DUCK...

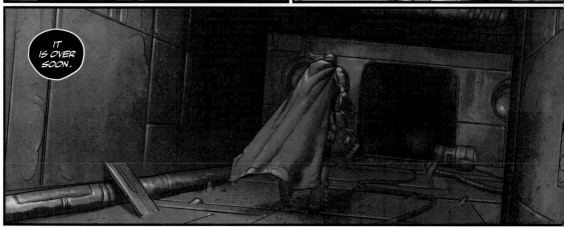

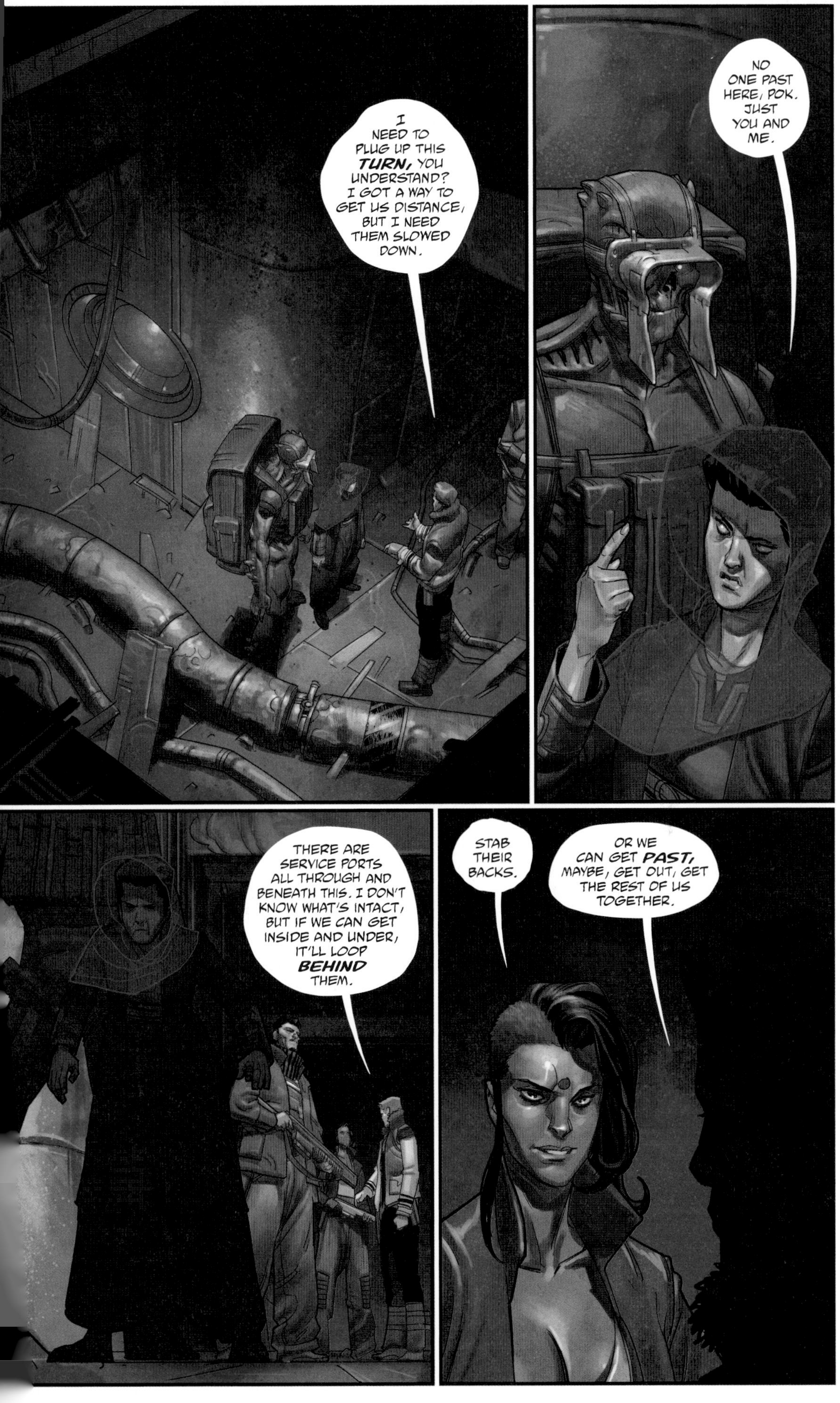
I NEED TO PLUG UP THIS TURN, YOU UNDERSTAND? I GOT A WAY TO GET US DISTANCE, BUT I NEED THEM SLOWED DOWN.
NO ONE PAST HERE, POK. JUST YOU AND ME.
THERE ARE SERVICE PORTS ALL THROUGH AND BENEATH THIS. I DON'T KNOW WHAT'S INTACT, BUT IF WE CAN GET INSIDE AND UNDER, IT'LL LOOP BEHIND THEM.
STAB THEIR BACKS.
OR WE CAN GET PAST, MAYBE, GET OUT, GET THE REST OF US TOGETHER.

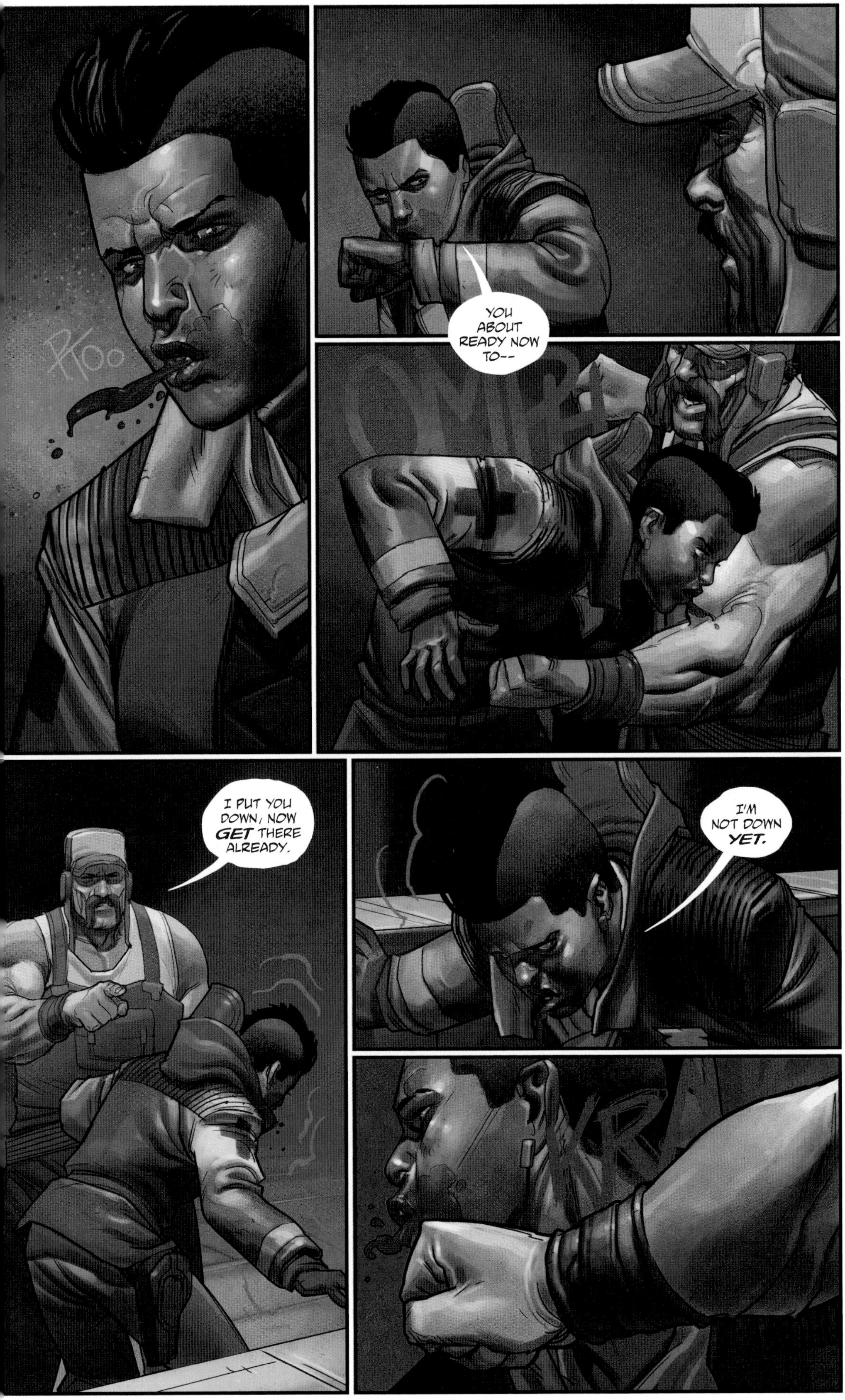
PTOO
YOU ABOUT READY NOW TO--
I PUT YOU DOWN, NOW GET THERE ALREADY.
I'M NOT DOWN YET.

SHOT THIS SAME FACE ONCE BEFORE AND STILL IT STARED AT ME.

WHY ARE YOU FOLLOWING US?

MAYBE UP HERE CLOSE AT LEAST IT HURTS.

WE ARE HERE. THIS IS WHERE WE LIVE.

RIGHT *HERE?* IN THE BROKEN GUTS OF MY SHIP?

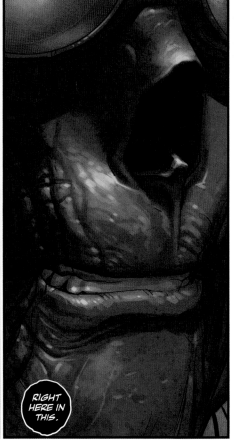

RIGHT HERE IN THIS.

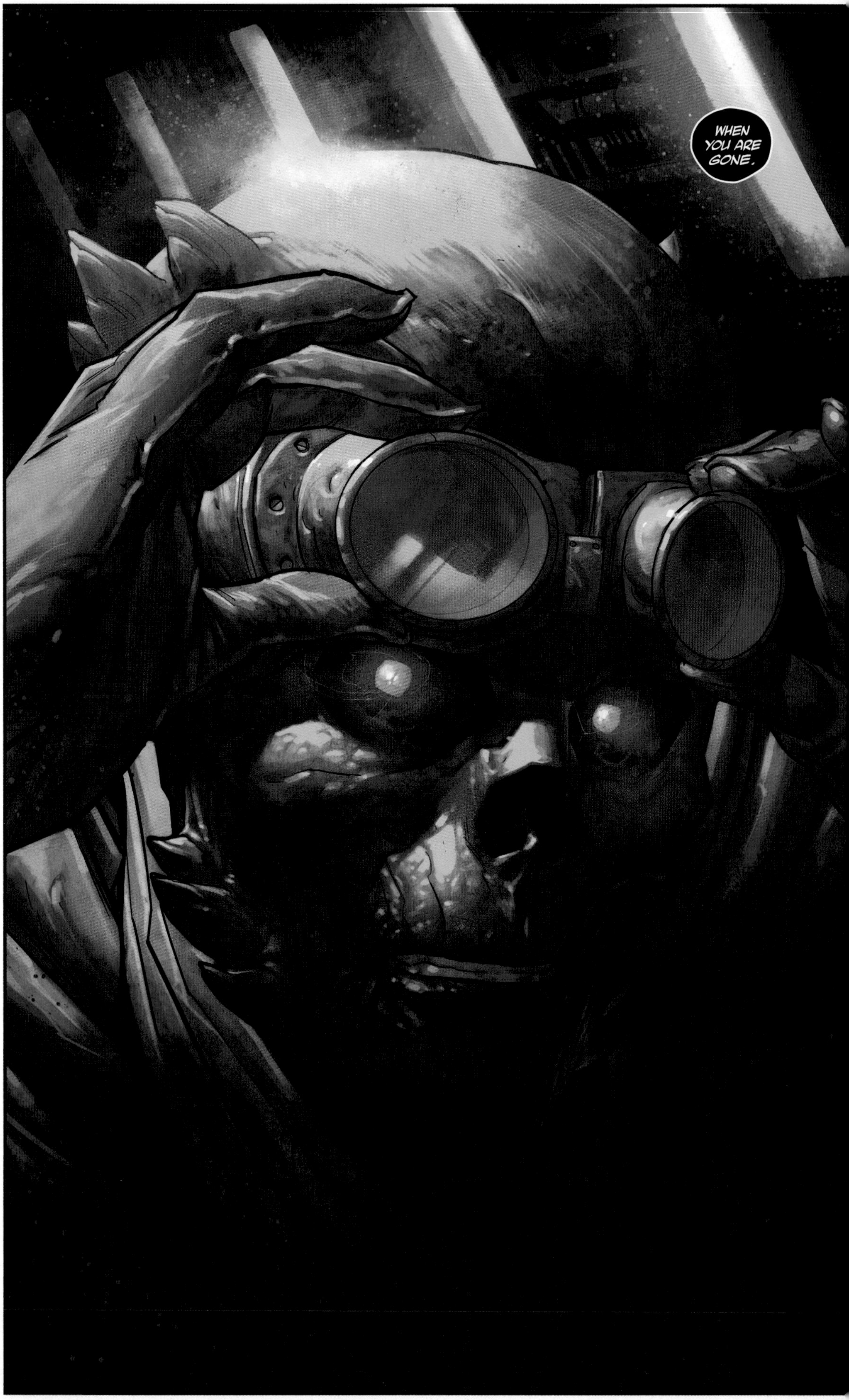
WHEN YOU ARE GONE.

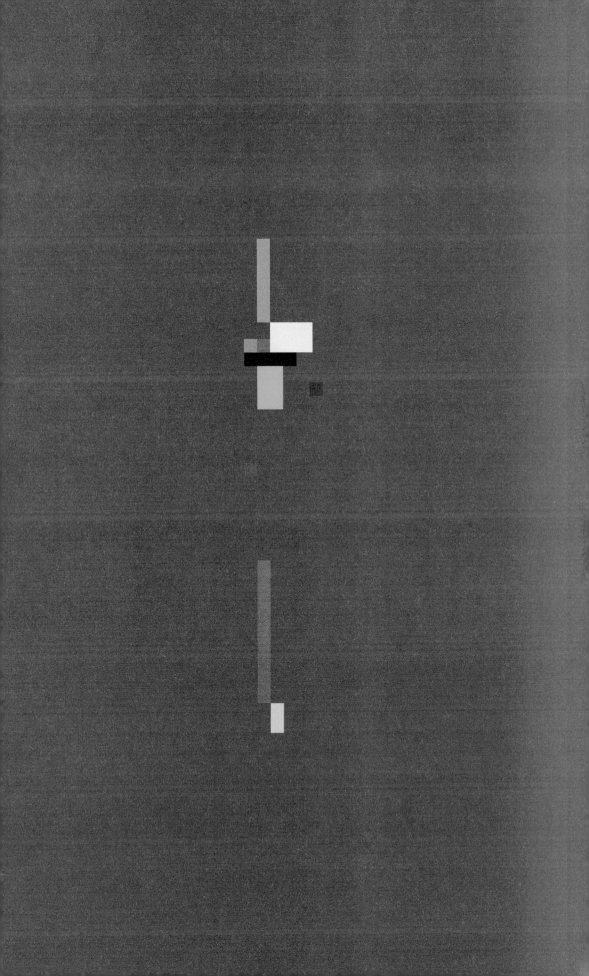

CHAPTER 9
424

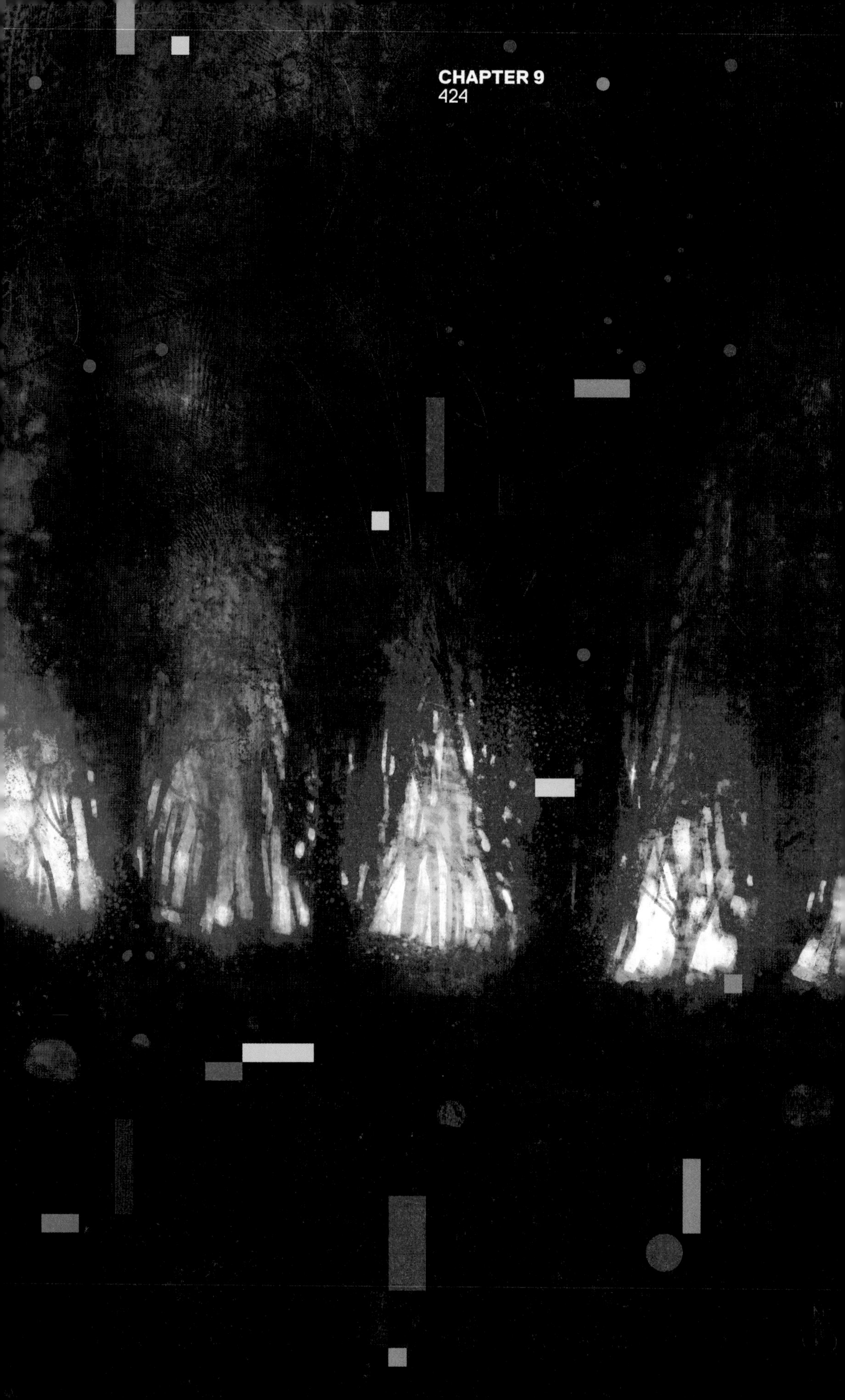

FELL AT EVERY STEP BUT STILL I TRIED TO WALK.

WE HAVE TO **THINK** NOW. **NOT** SPEAK. IF WE ARE WRONG, WE LOSE IT ALL.

EACH TIME THAT LINE IT PULLED AT ME.

WHOLE **TRUCK** FULL OF FRIENDLIES DOWN THE WAY. BRING THEM BACK HERE AND YOU CAN STORM THE GATES **TOGETHER.**

LIKE YOU WERE PULLING ME TO STAND AGAIN.

WE HAVE ZERO TIME FOR THIS.

WE'LL BE SUPERFAST.

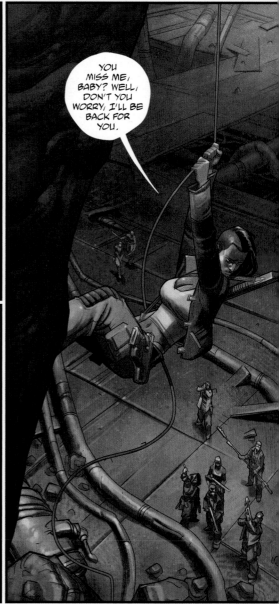

YOU MISS ME, BABY? WELL, DON'T YOU WORRY, I'LL BE BACK FOR YOU.

PULLING ME A LITTLE CLOSER.

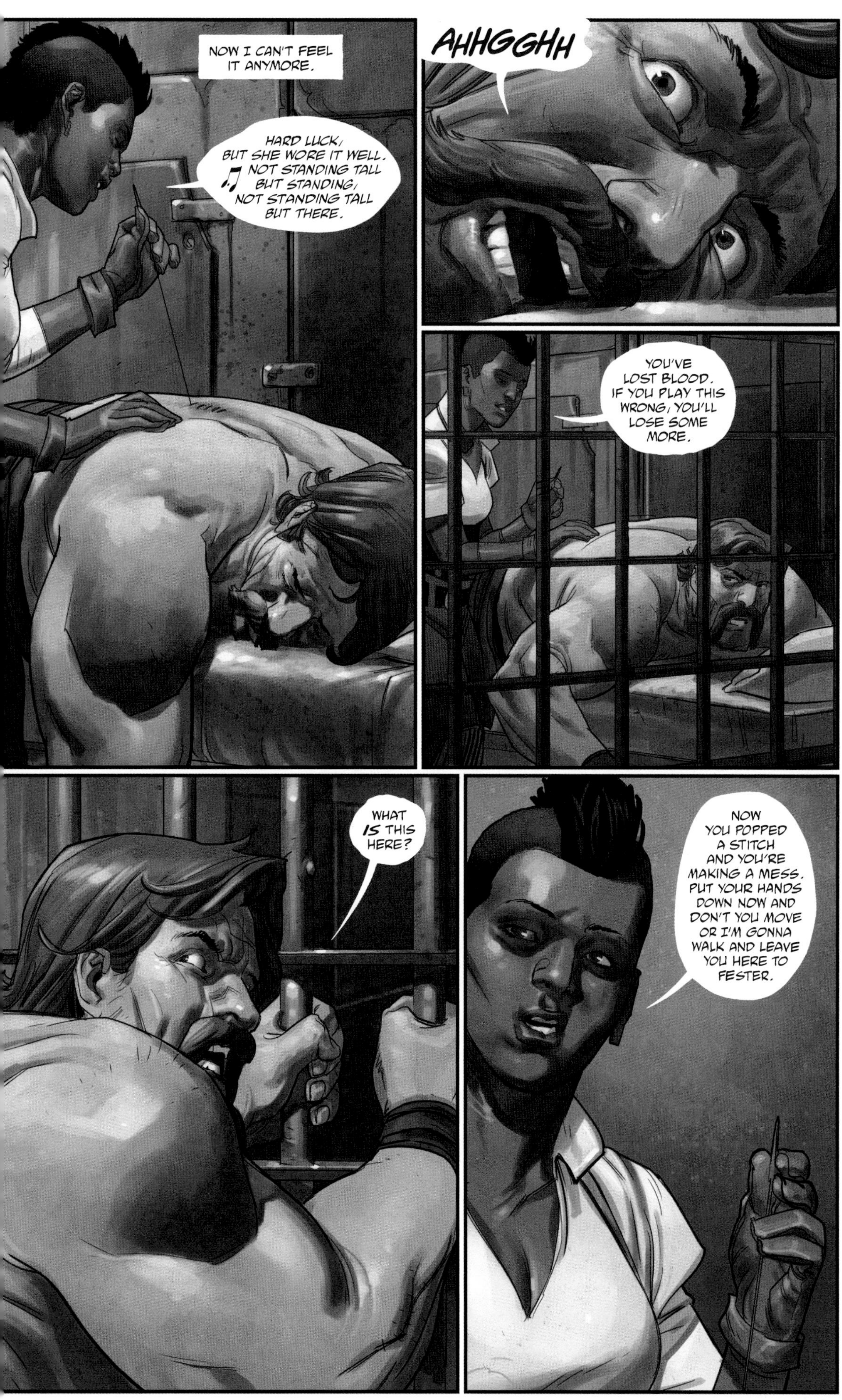NOW I CAN'T FEEL IT ANYMORE.
HARD LUCK, BUT SHE WORE IT WELL. NOT STANDING TALL BUT STANDING, NOT STANDING TALL BUT THERE.
AHHGGHH
YOU'VE LOST BLOOD. IF YOU PLAY THIS WRONG, YOU'LL LOSE SOME MORE.
WHAT IS THIS HERE?
NOW YOU POPPED A STITCH AND YOU'RE MAKING A MESS. PUT YOUR HANDS DOWN NOW AND DON'T YOU MOVE OR I'M GONNA WALK AND LEAVE YOU HERE TO FESTER.

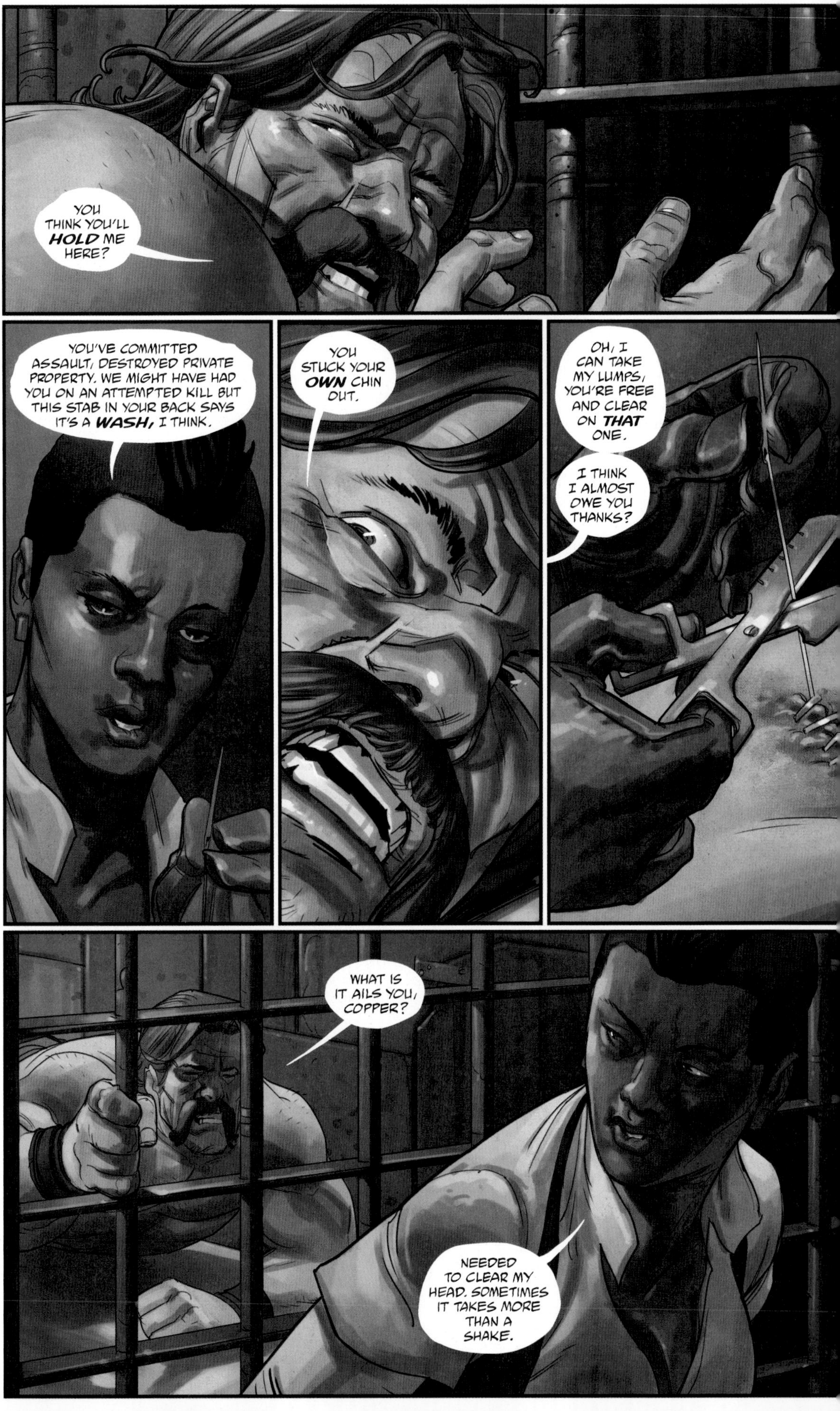
YOU THINK YOU'LL **HOLD** ME HERE?
YOU'VE COMMITTED ASSAULT, DESTROYED PRIVATE PROPERTY. WE MIGHT HAVE HAD YOU ON AN ATTEMPTED KILL BUT THIS STAB IN YOUR BACK SAYS IT'S A **WASH,** I THINK.
YOU STUCK YOUR **OWN** CHIN OUT.
OH, I CAN TAKE MY LUMPS, YOU'RE FREE AND CLEAR ON **THAT** ONE.
I THINK I ALMOST OWE YOU THANKS?
WHAT IS IT AILS YOU, COPPER?
NEEDED TO CLEAR MY HEAD. SOMETIMES IT TAKES MORE THAN A SHAKE.

I SET MY TEETH TO DIE. IT'S WHAT I'M GOOD AT.

I DON'T KNOW WHAT IT IS THAT PUTS YOU AT MY THROAT, BUT I DIDN'T COME HERE TO KILL THEM WHO ATTACKED ME.

WITHOUT YOUR PULL, I TRY FOR ANGER. BUT I'M ALONE.

I SENT OUR PEOPLE THIS WAY TO *ESCAPE.* NOT TO FIGHT. TO GET *PAST* YOU AND *OUT.*

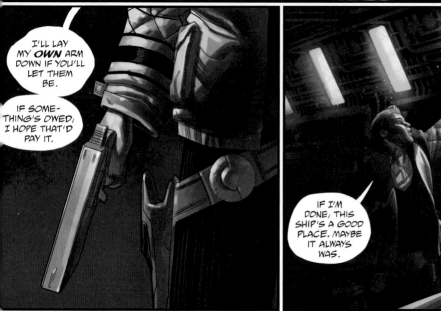

I'LL LAY MY *OWN* ARM DOWN IF YOU'LL LET THEM BE.

IF SOMETHING'S OWED, I HOPE THAT'D PAY IT.

IF I'M DONE, THIS SHIP'S A GOOD PLACE. MAYBE IT ALWAYS WAS.

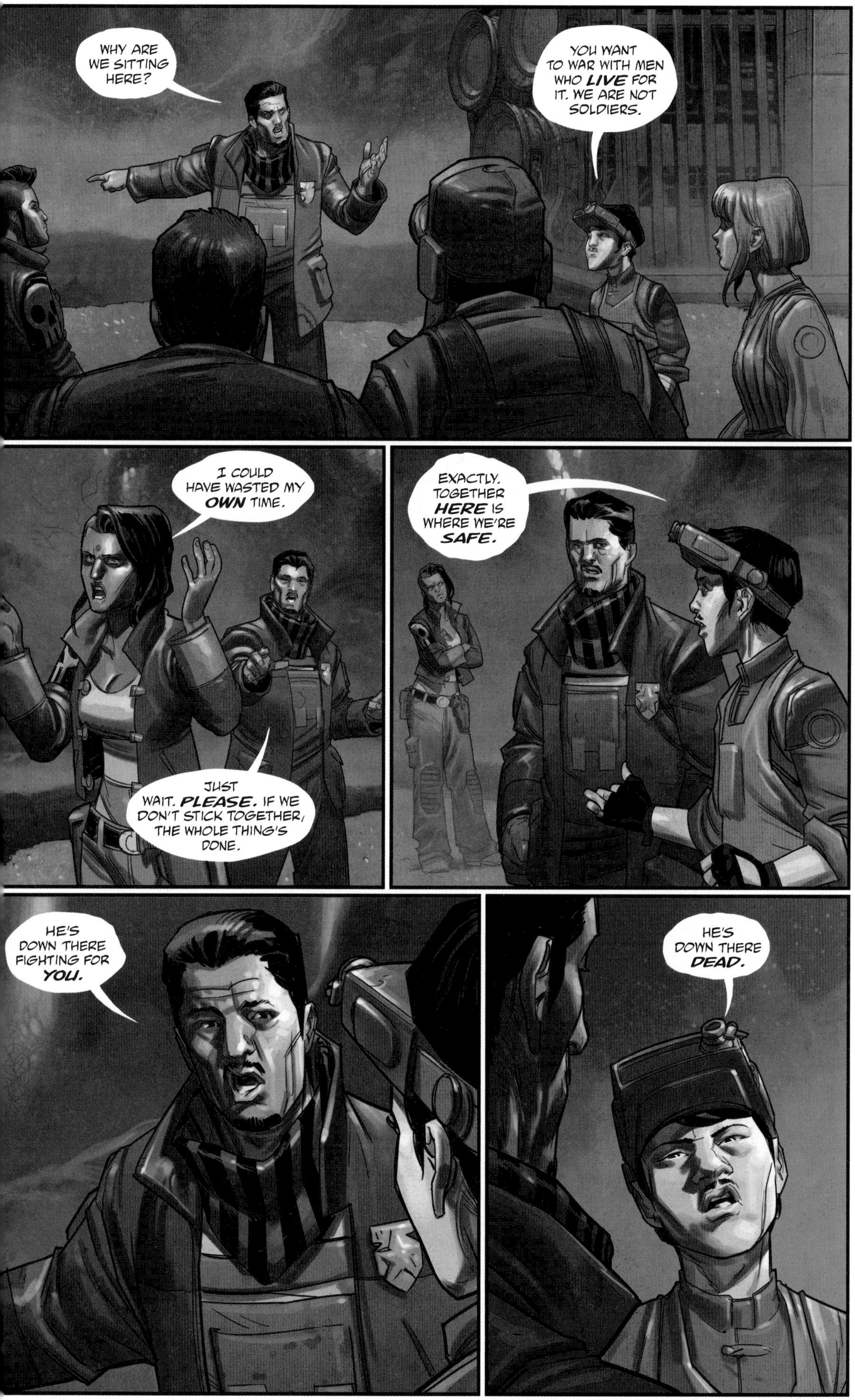
WHY ARE WE SITTING HERE?
YOU WANT TO WAR WITH MEN WHO LIVE FOR IT. WE ARE NOT SOLDIERS.
I COULD HAVE WASTED MY OWN TIME.
JUST WAIT. PLEASE. IF WE DON'T STICK TOGETHER, THE WHOLE THING'S DONE.
EXACTLY. TOGETHER HERE IS WHERE WE'RE SAFE.
HE'S DOWN THERE FIGHTING FOR YOU.
HE'S DOWN THERE DEAD.

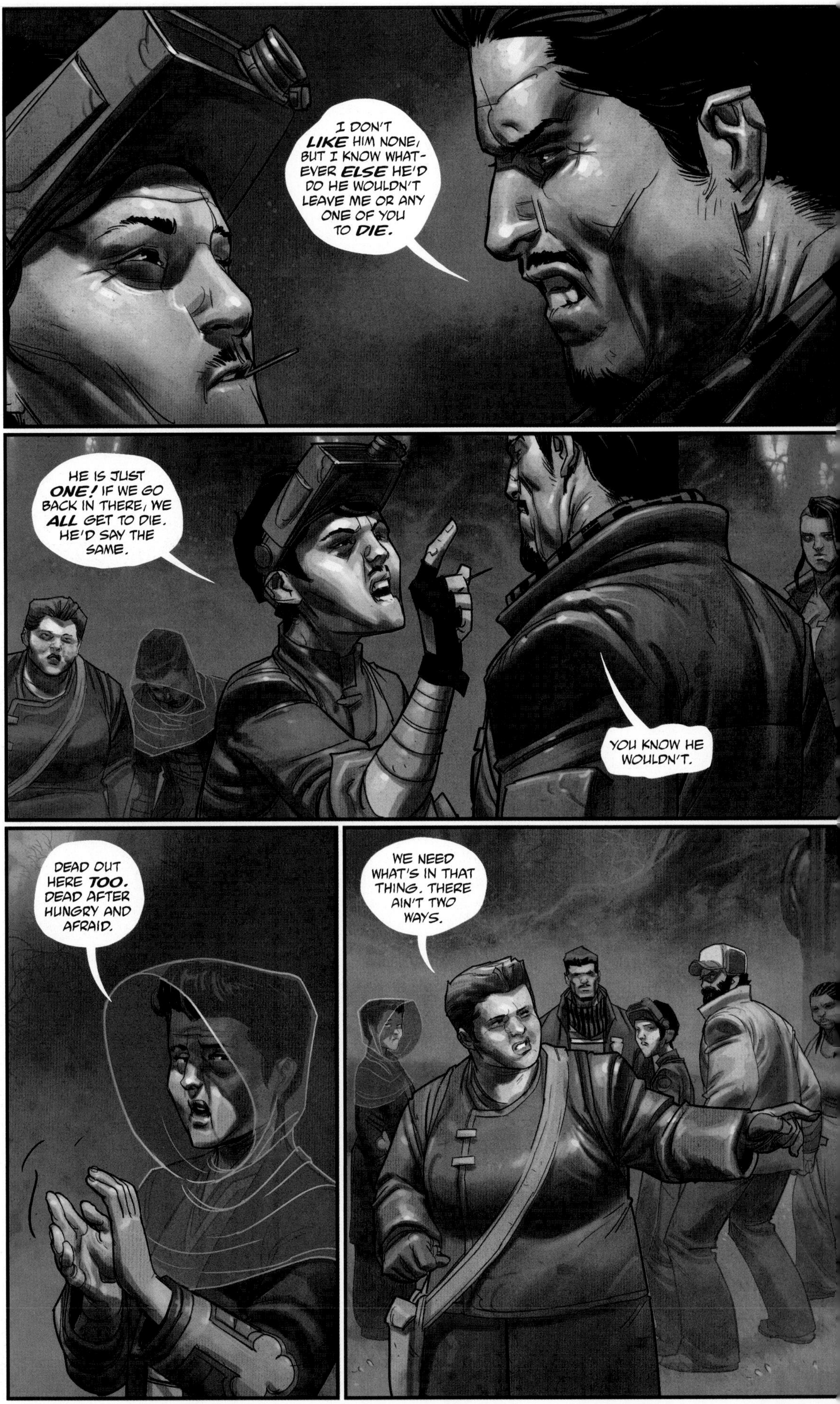
I DON'T **LIKE** HIM NONE, BUT I KNOW WHAT-EVER **ELSE** HE'D DO HE WOULDN'T LEAVE ME OR ANY ONE OF YOU TO **DIE.**
HE IS JUST **ONE!** IF WE GO BACK IN THERE, WE **ALL** GET TO DIE. HE'D SAY THE SAME.
YOU KNOW HE WOULDN'T.
DEAD OUT HERE **TOO.** DEAD AFTER HUNGRY AND AFRAID.
WE NEED WHAT'S IN THAT THING. THERE AIN'T TWO WAYS.

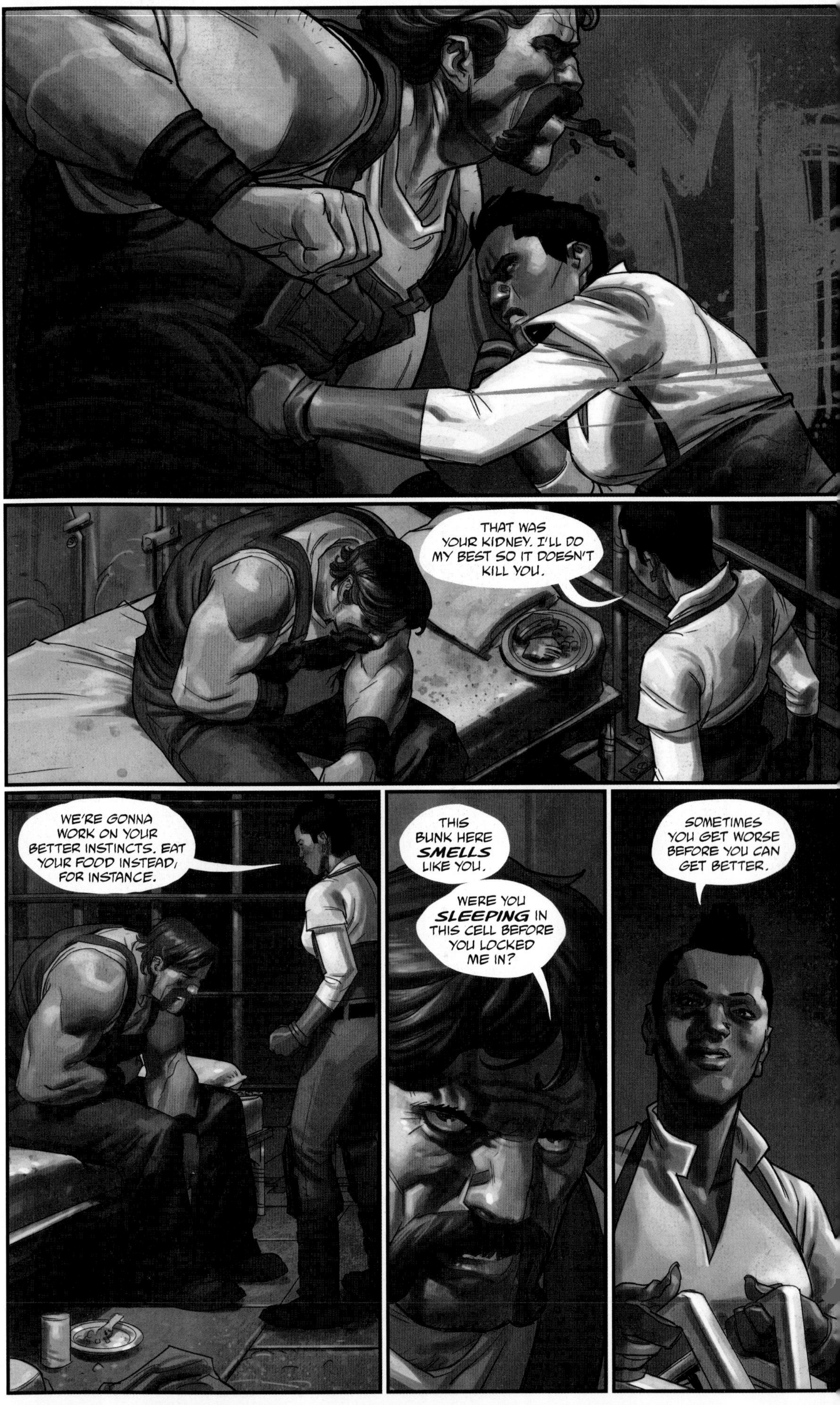
THAT WAS YOUR KIDNEY. I'LL DO MY BEST SO IT DOESN'T KILL YOU.
WE'RE GONNA WORK ON YOUR BETTER INSTINCTS. EAT YOUR FOOD INSTEAD, FOR INSTANCE.
THIS BUNK HERE SMELLS LIKE YOU.
WERE YOU SLEEPING IN THIS CELL BEFORE YOU LOCKED ME IN?
SOMETIMES YOU GET WORSE BEFORE YOU CAN GET BETTER.

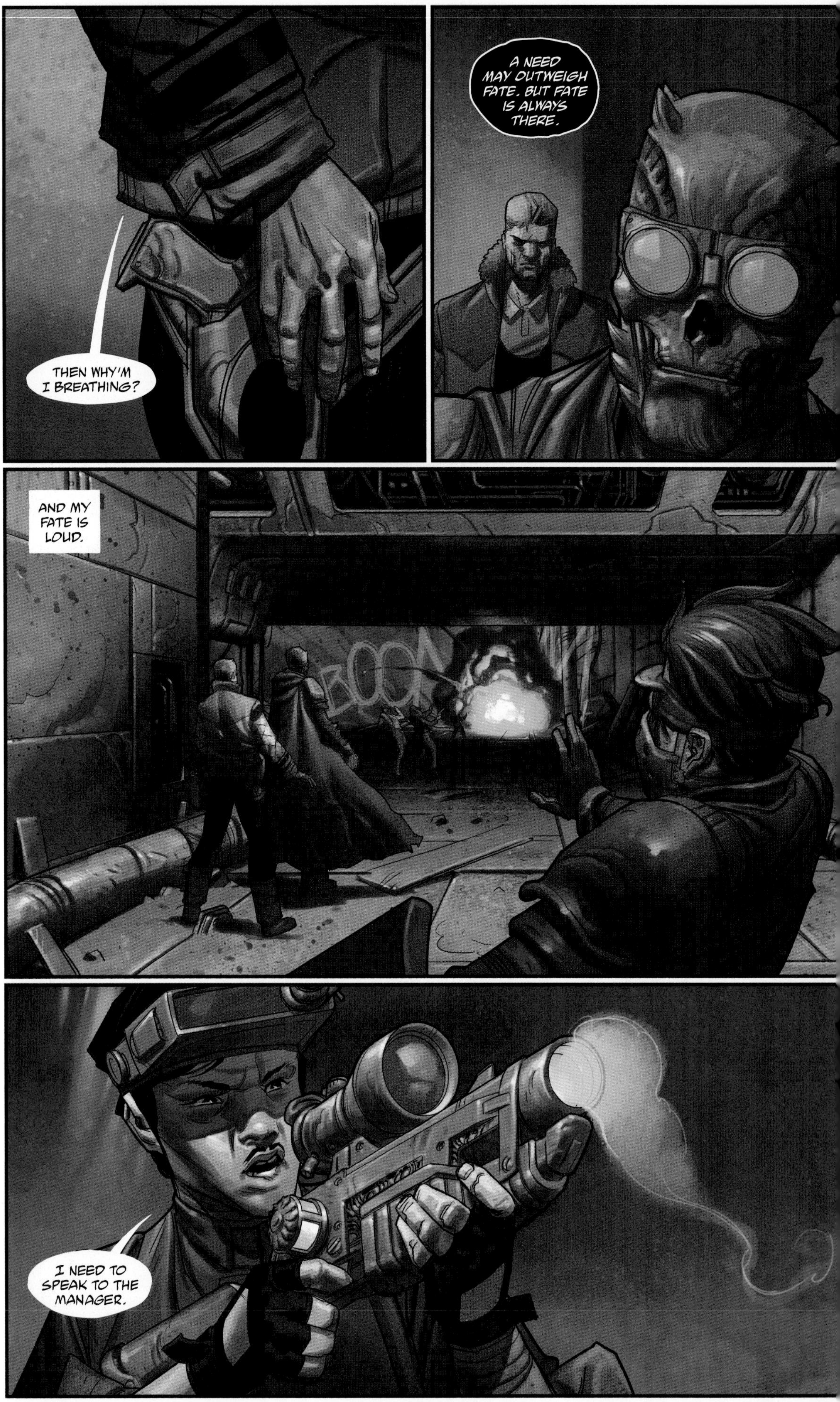

THEN WHY'M I BREATHING?
A NEED MAY OUTWEIGH FATE. BUT FATE IS ALWAYS THERE.
AND MY FATE IS LOUD.
BOOM
I NEED TO SPEAK TO THE MANAGER.

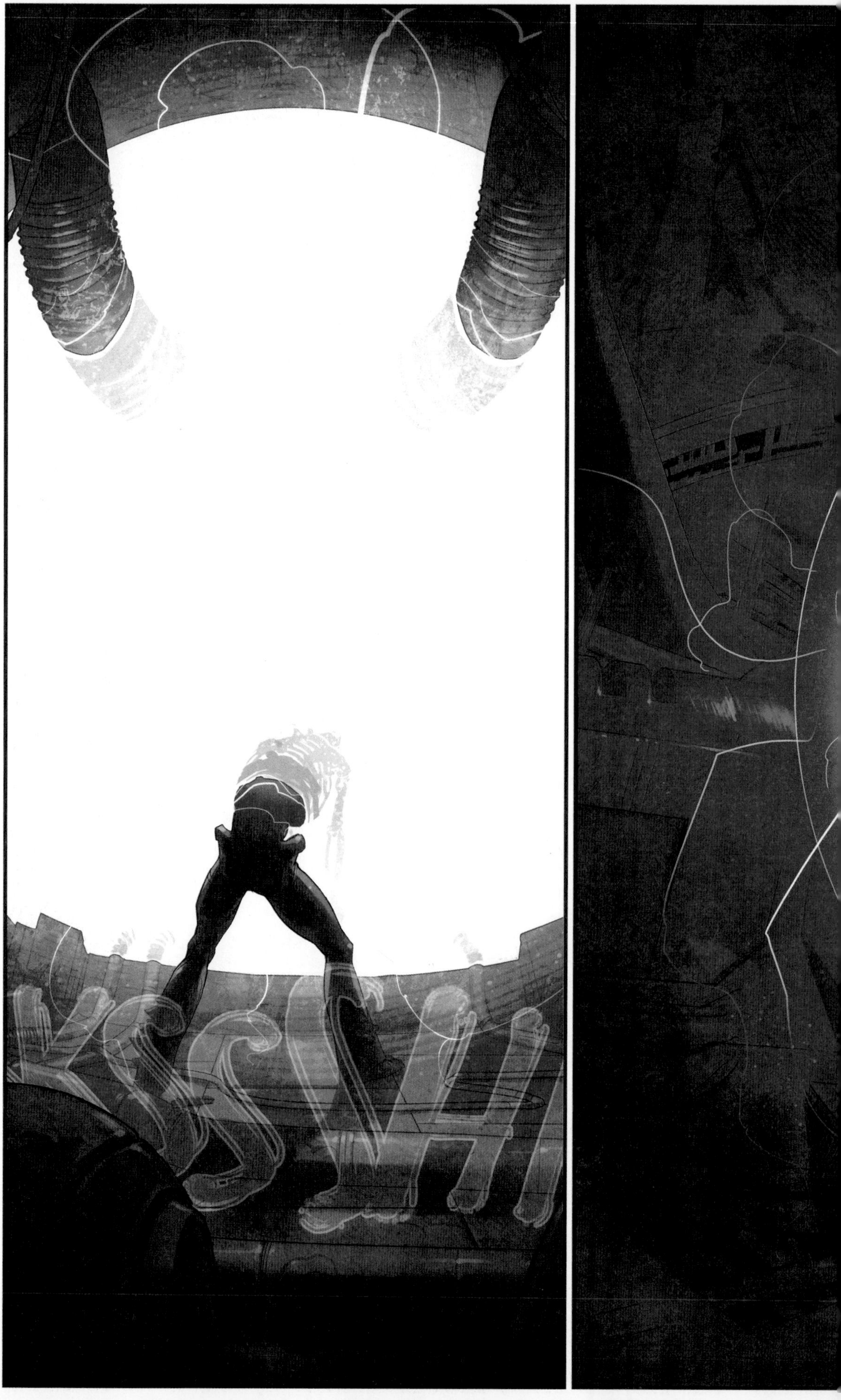

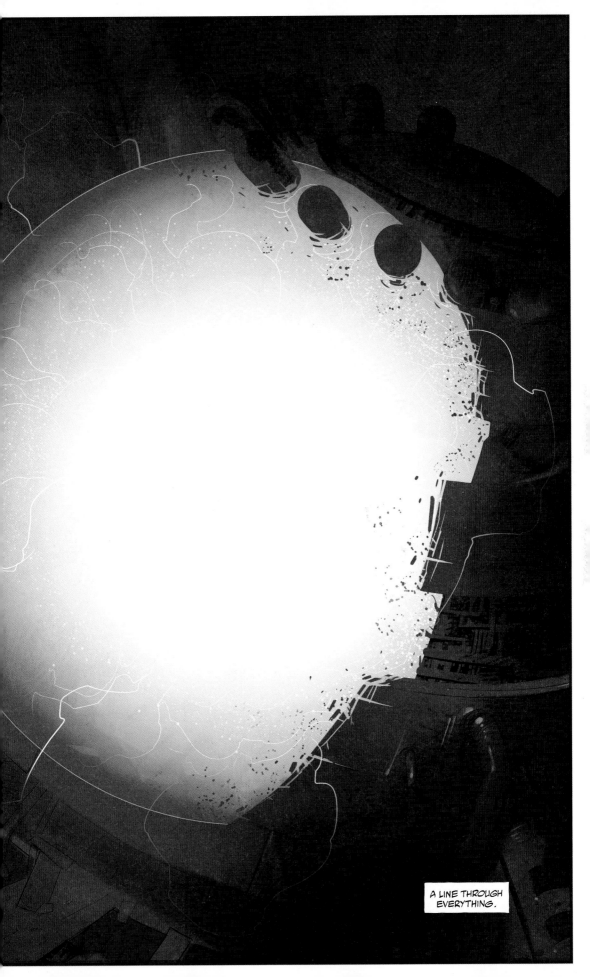

A LINE THROUGH EVERYTHING.

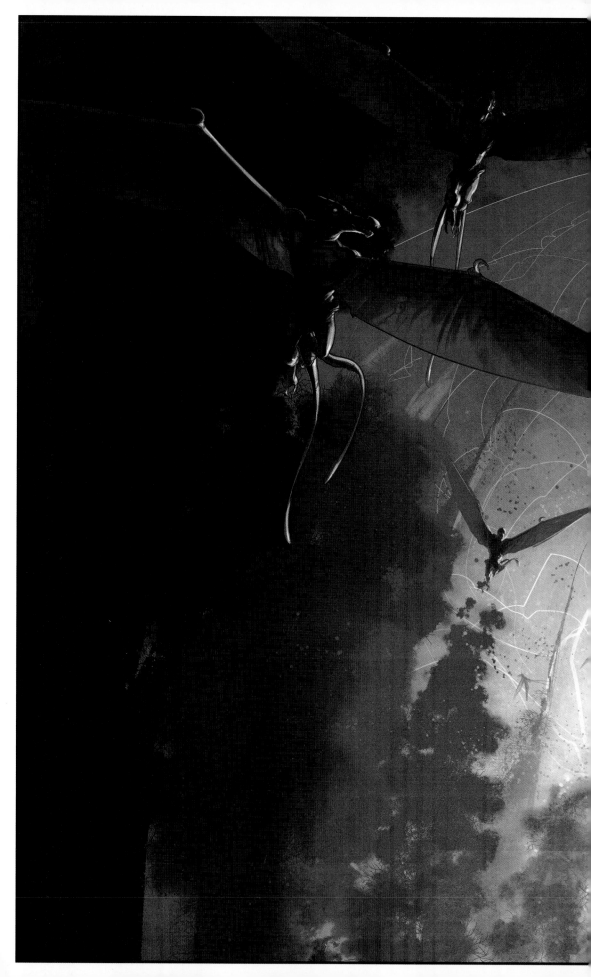

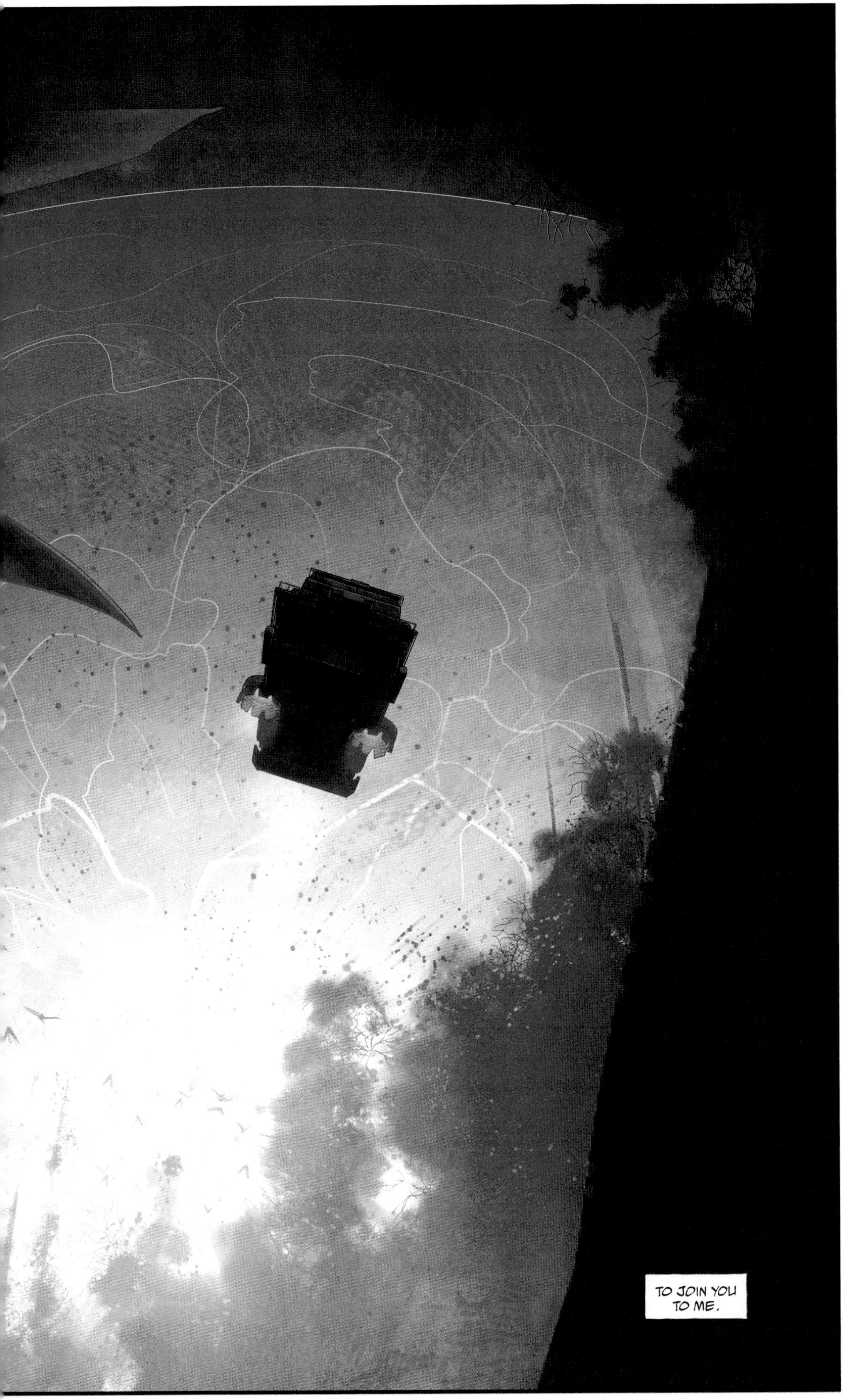
TO JOIN YOU
TO ME.

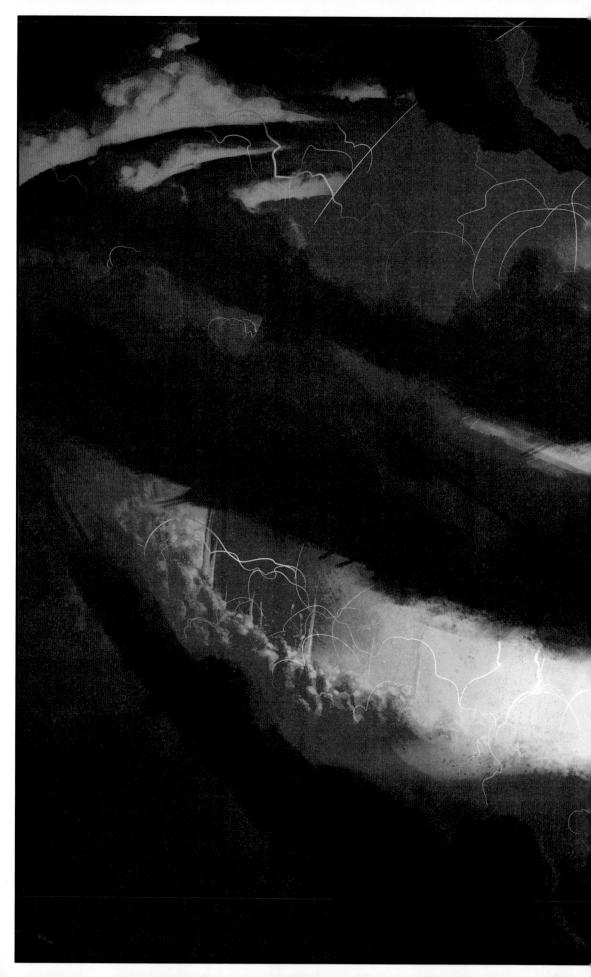

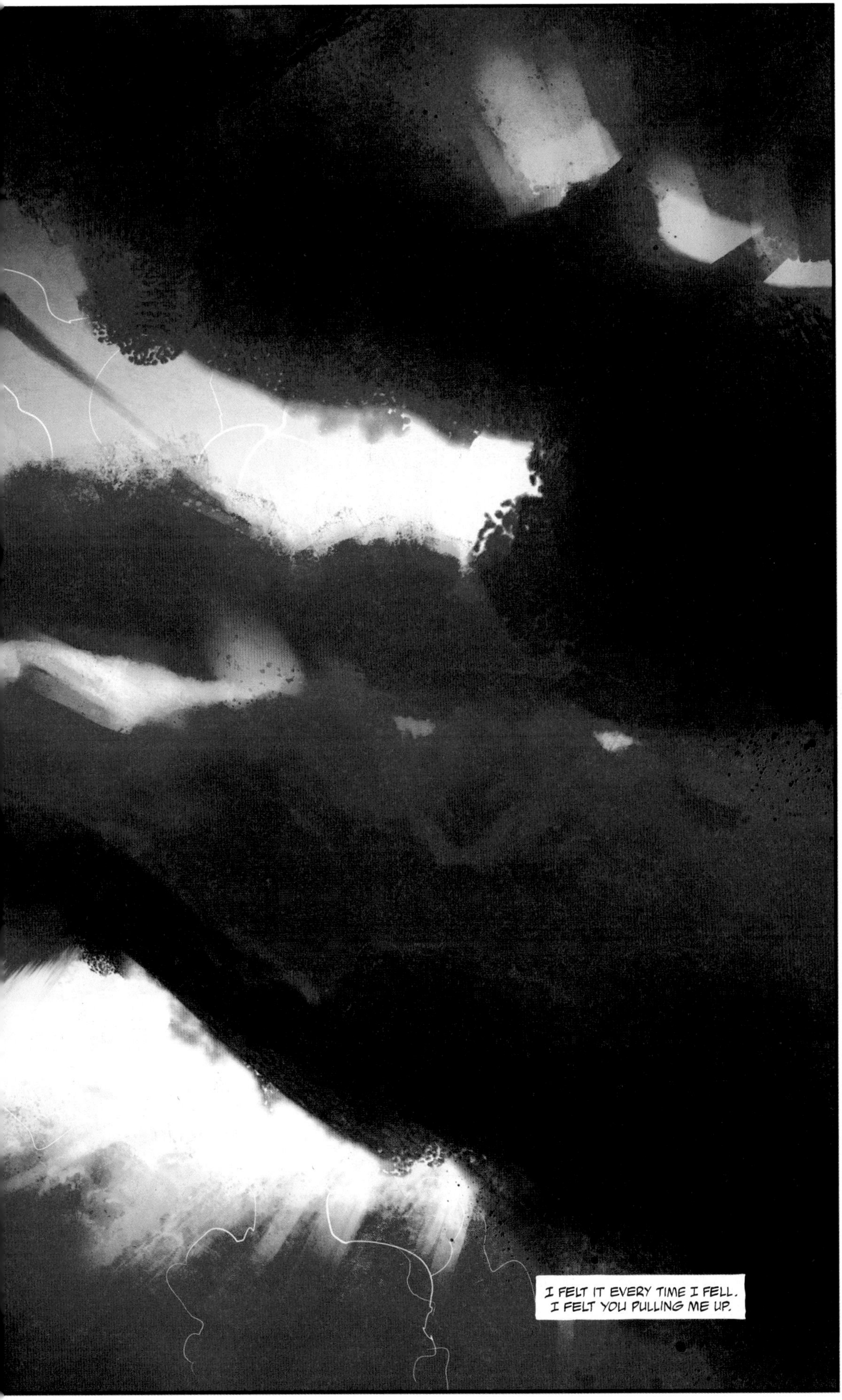
I FELT IT EVERY TIME I FELL. I FELT YOU PULLING ME UP.

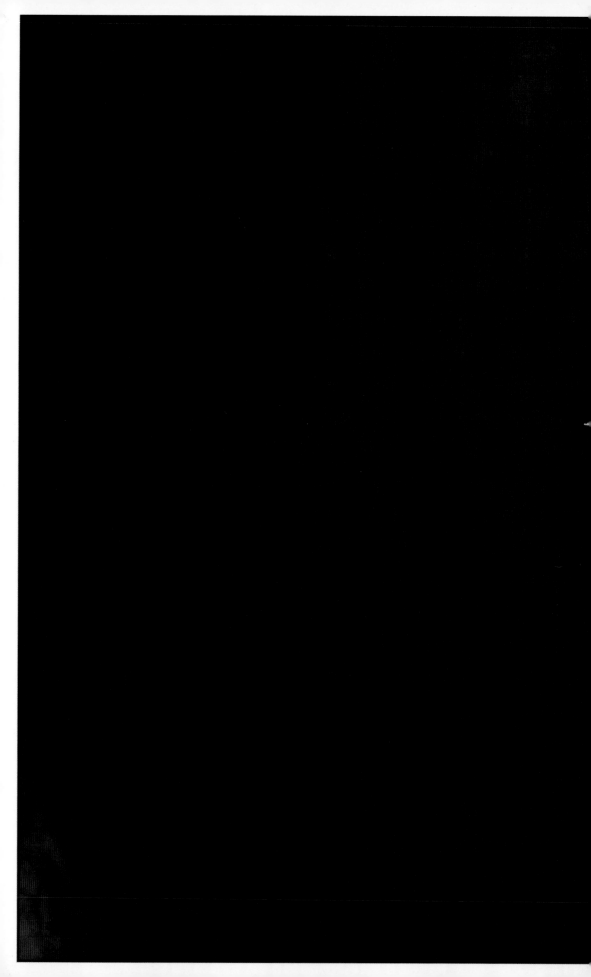

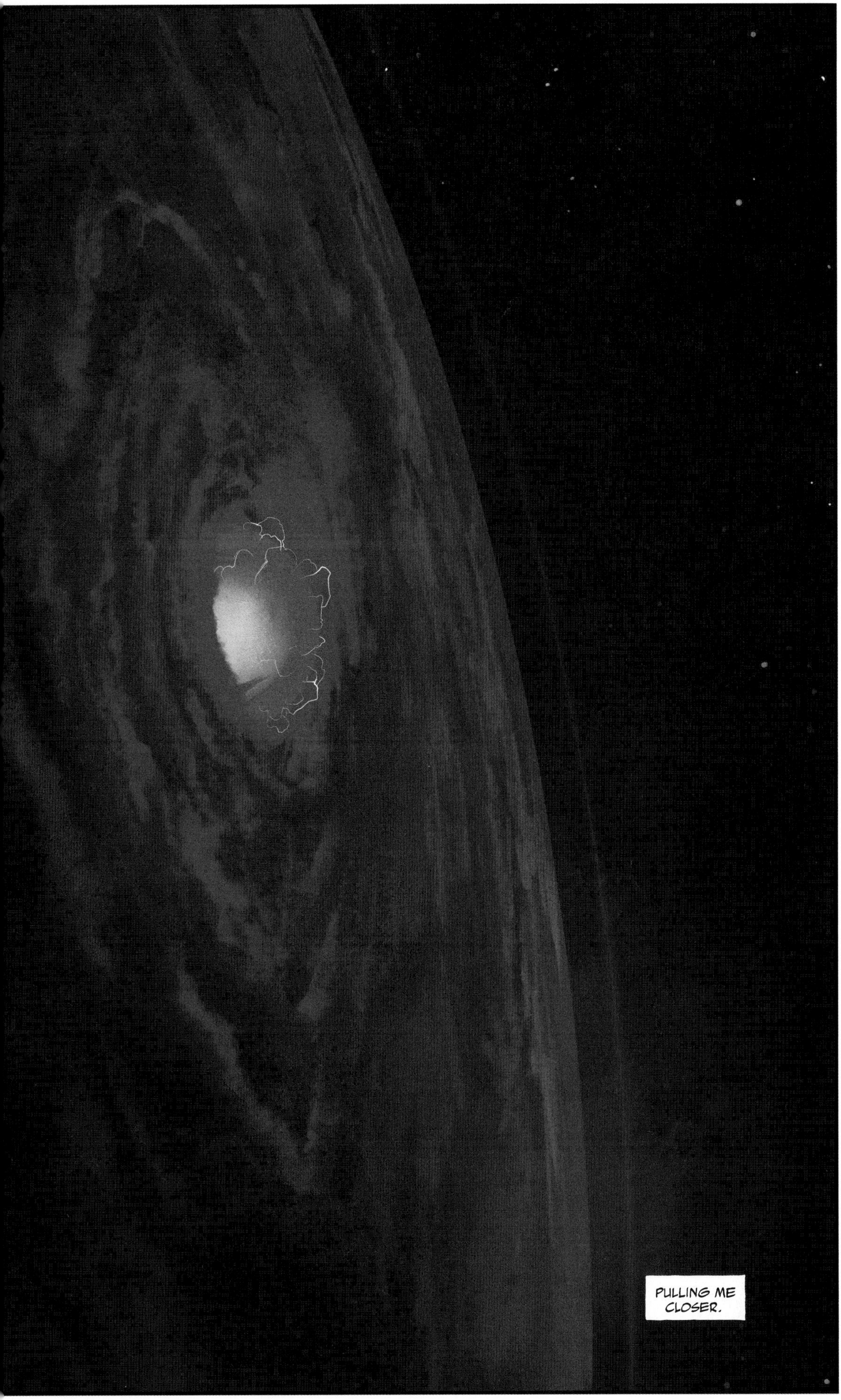
PULLING ME
CLOSER.

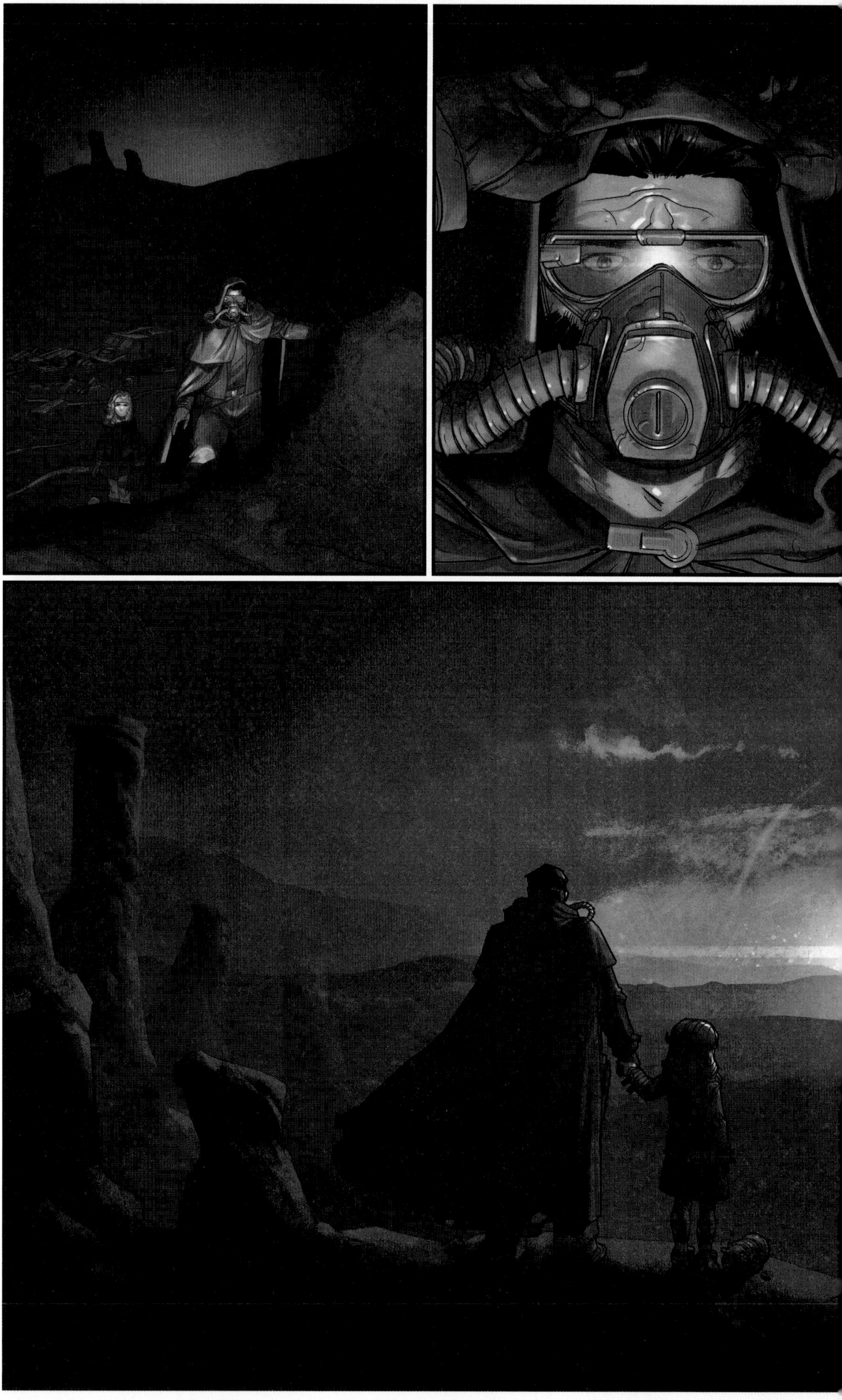

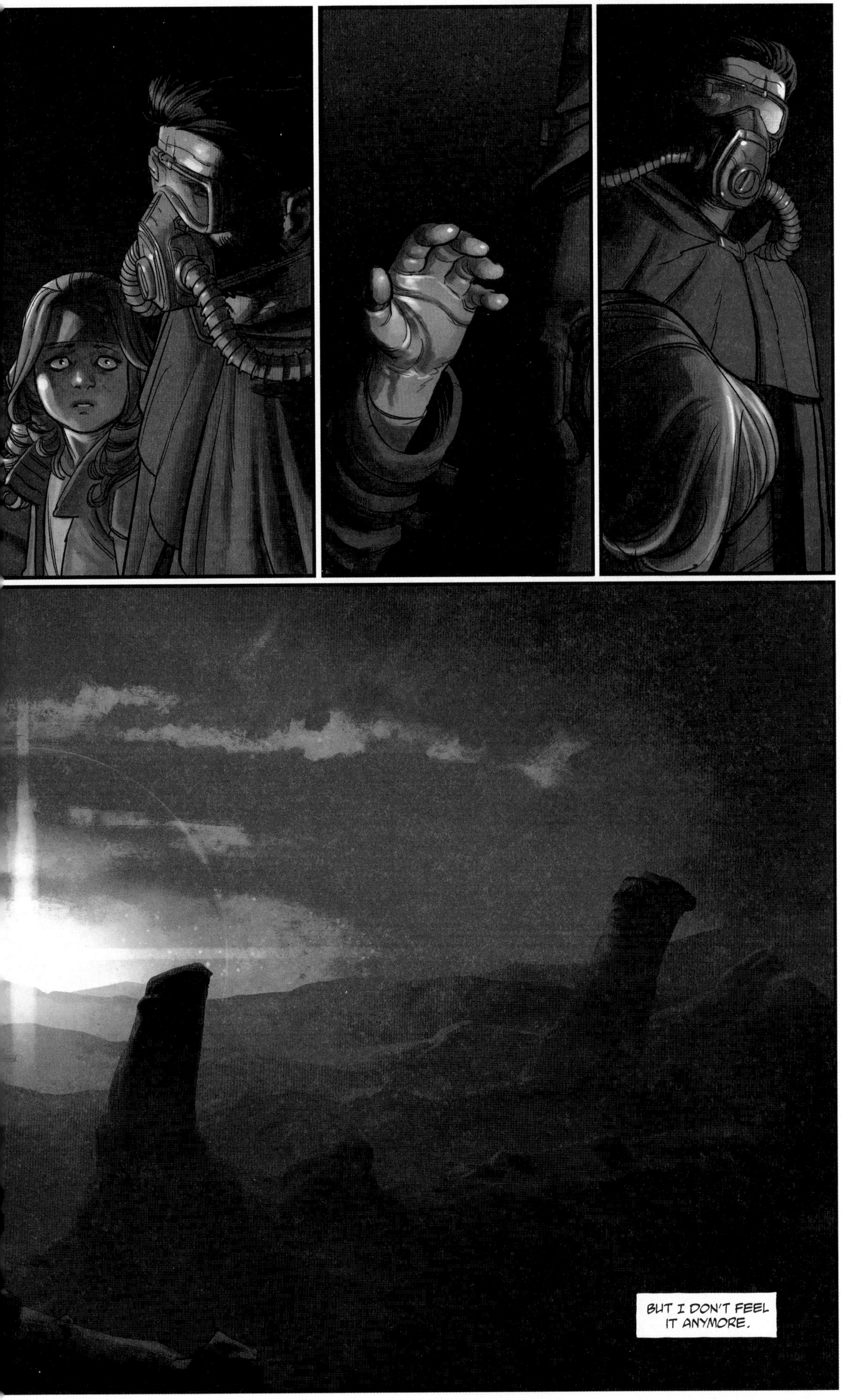
BUT I DON'T FEEL IT ANYMORE.

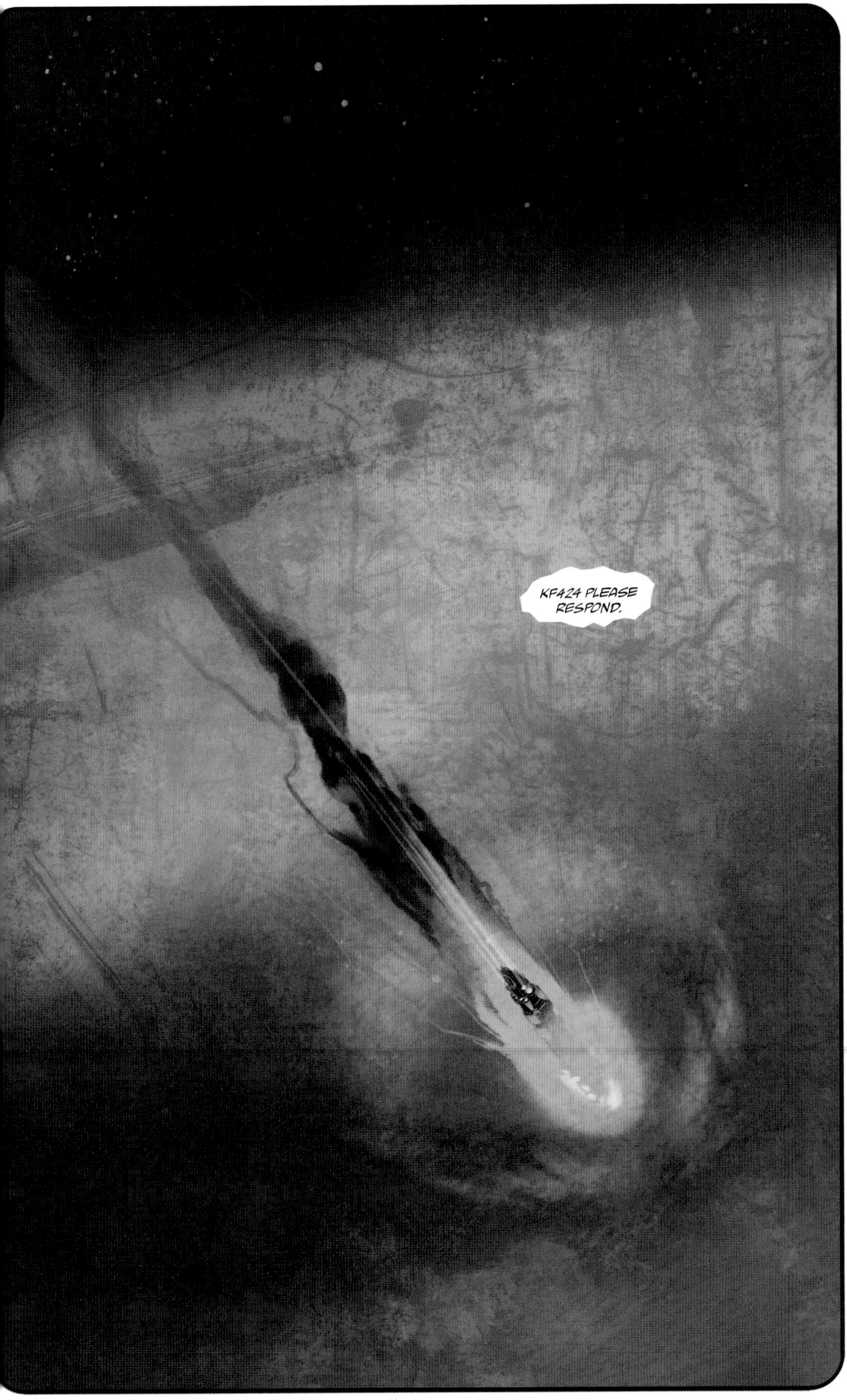
KF424 PLEASE RESPOND.

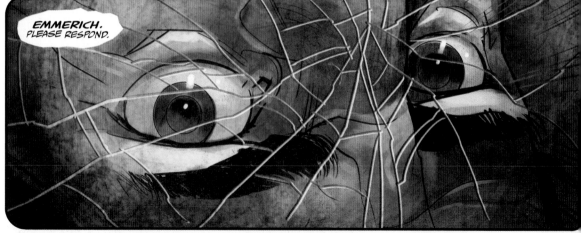

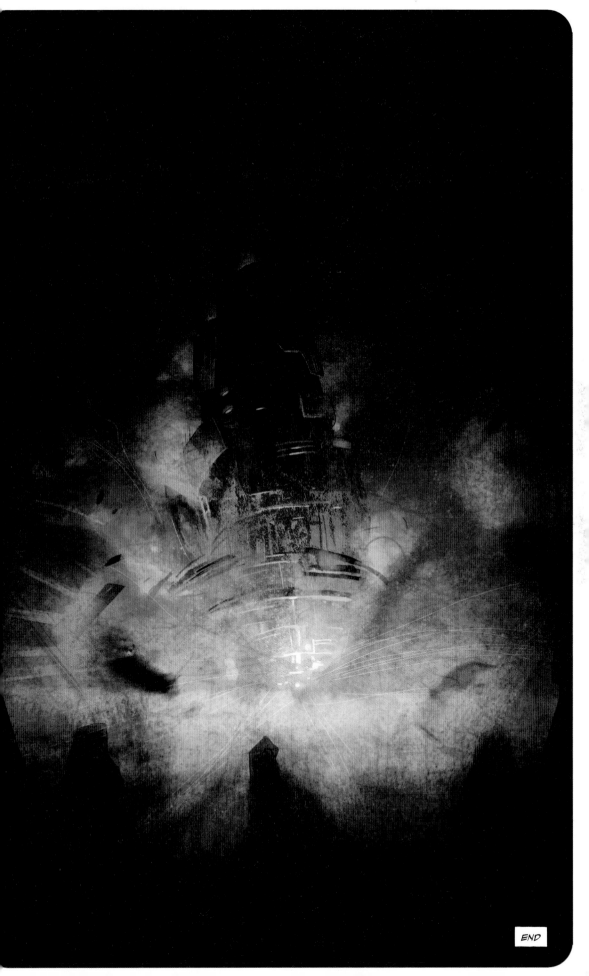

END

COVER GALLERY

Eduardo Risso, Tom Muller,
Daniel Krall, and Paul Azaceta

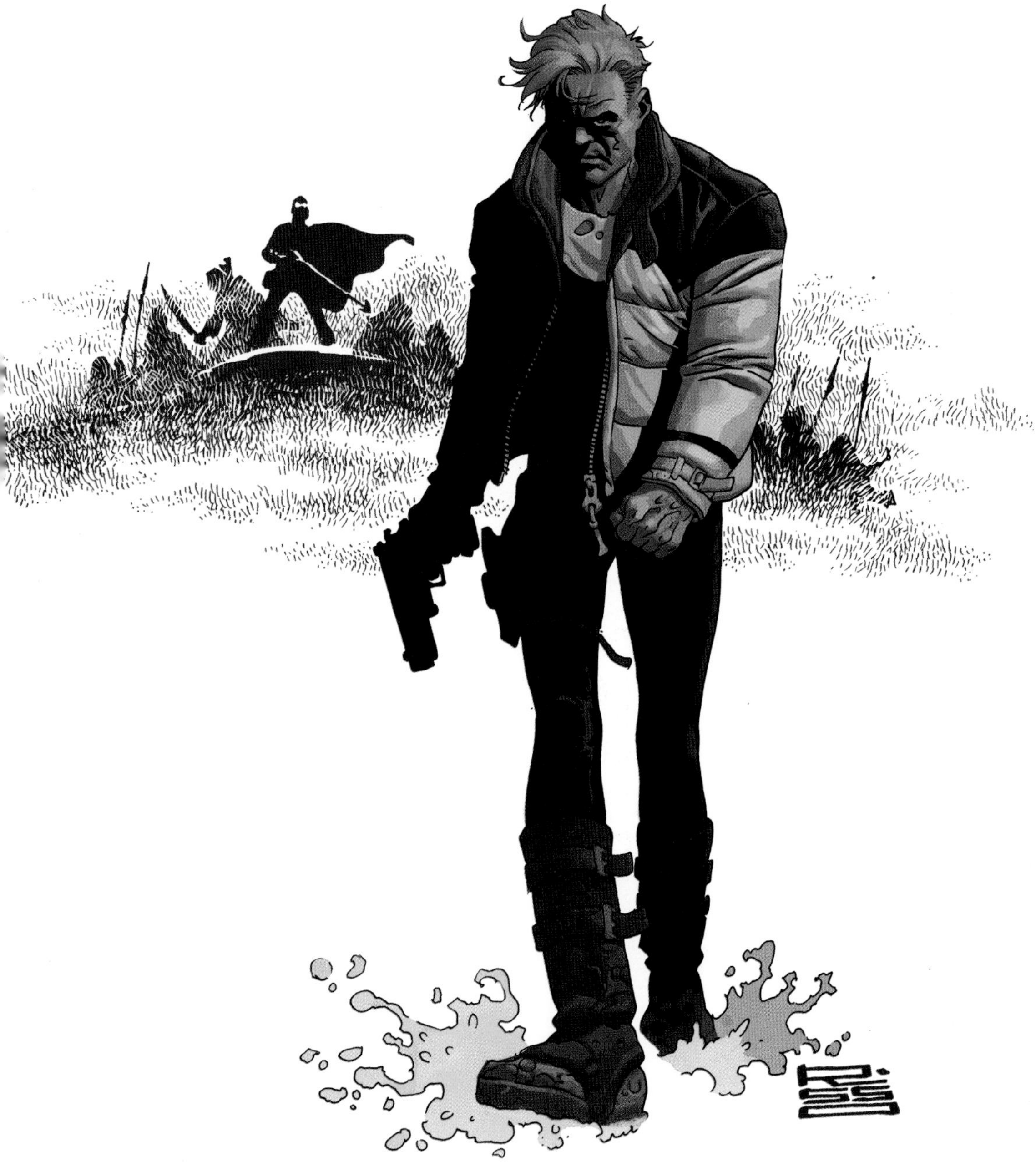

Eduardo Risso

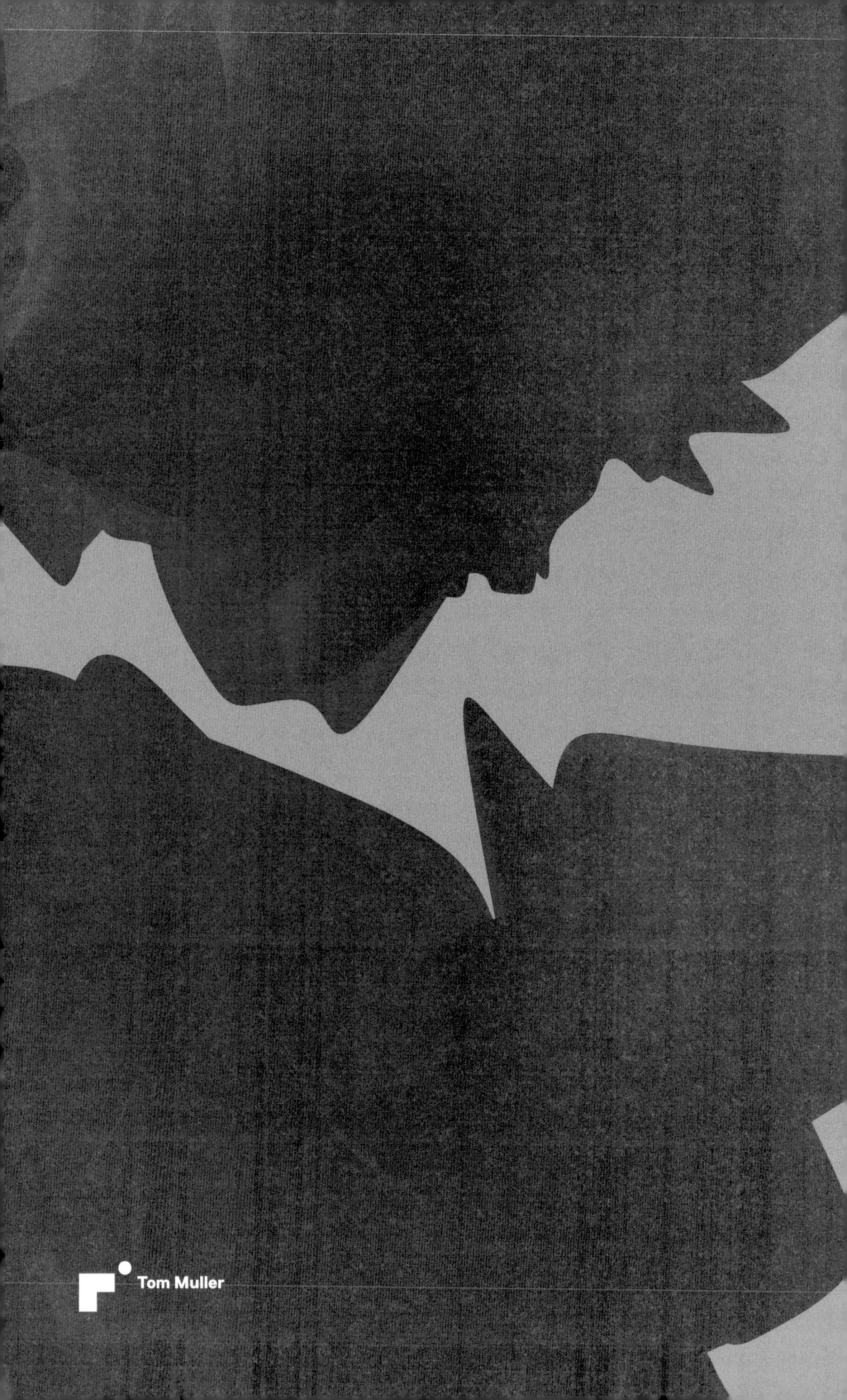
Tom Muller

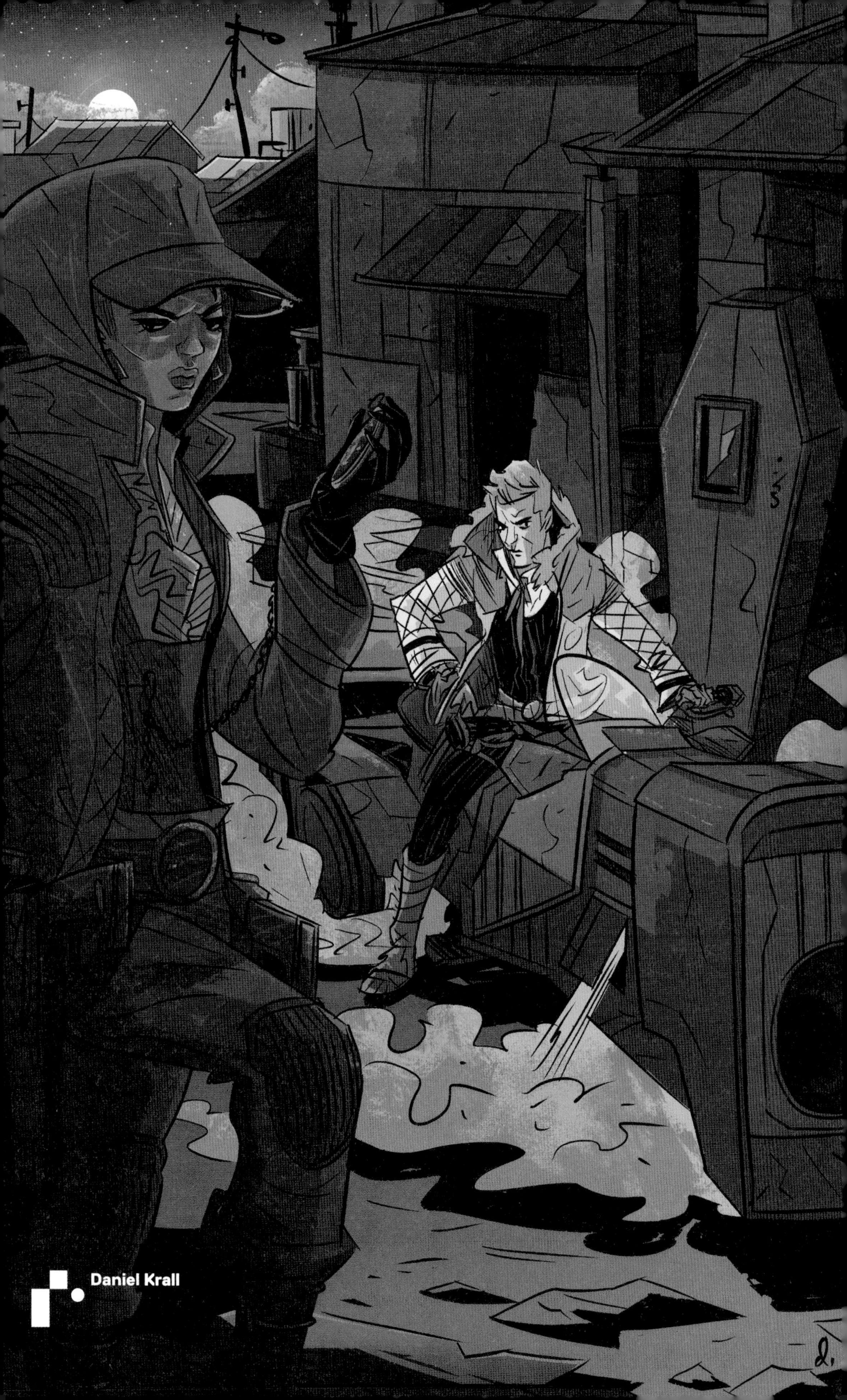

Daniel Krall

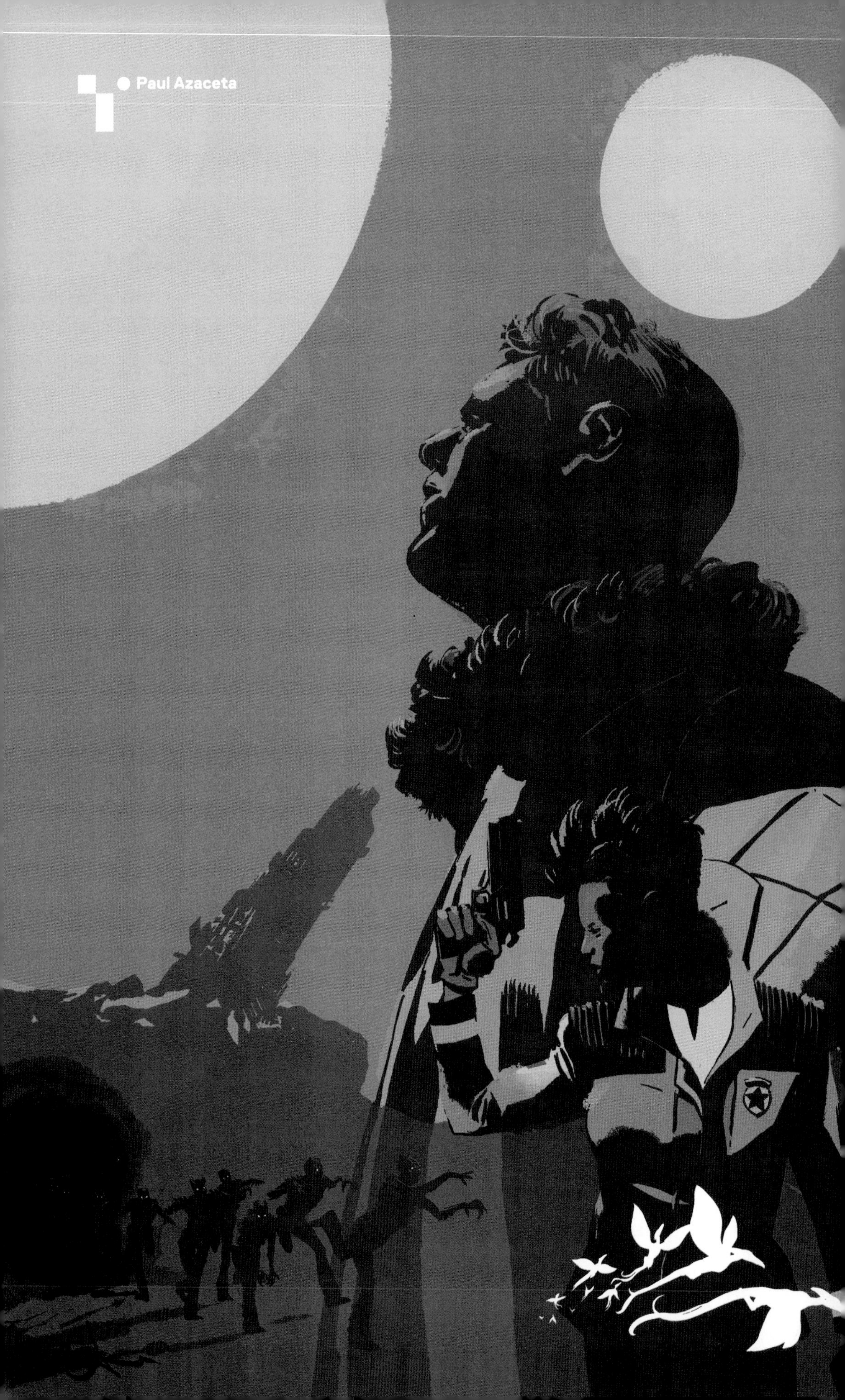

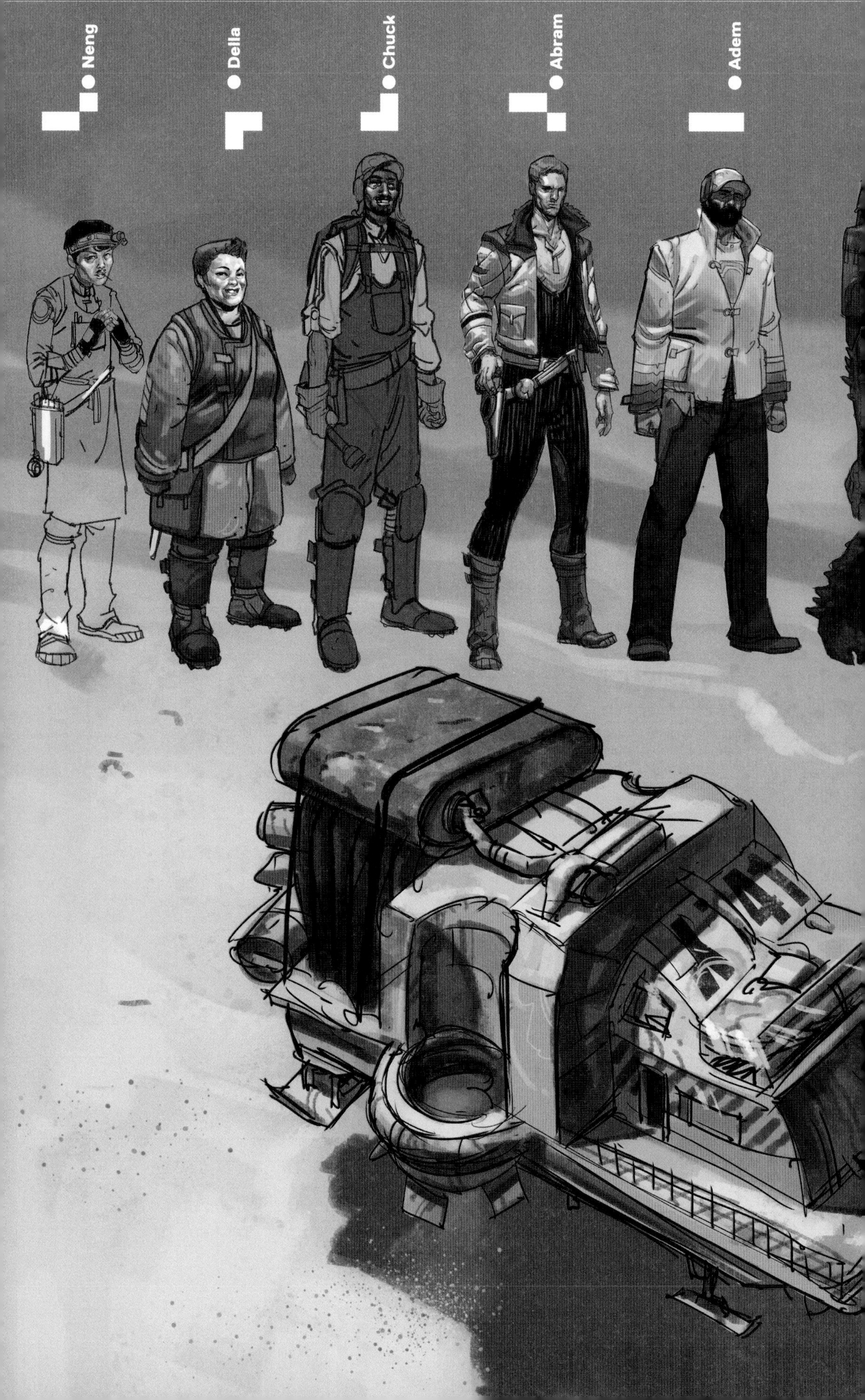
Neng
Della
Chuck
Abram
Adem

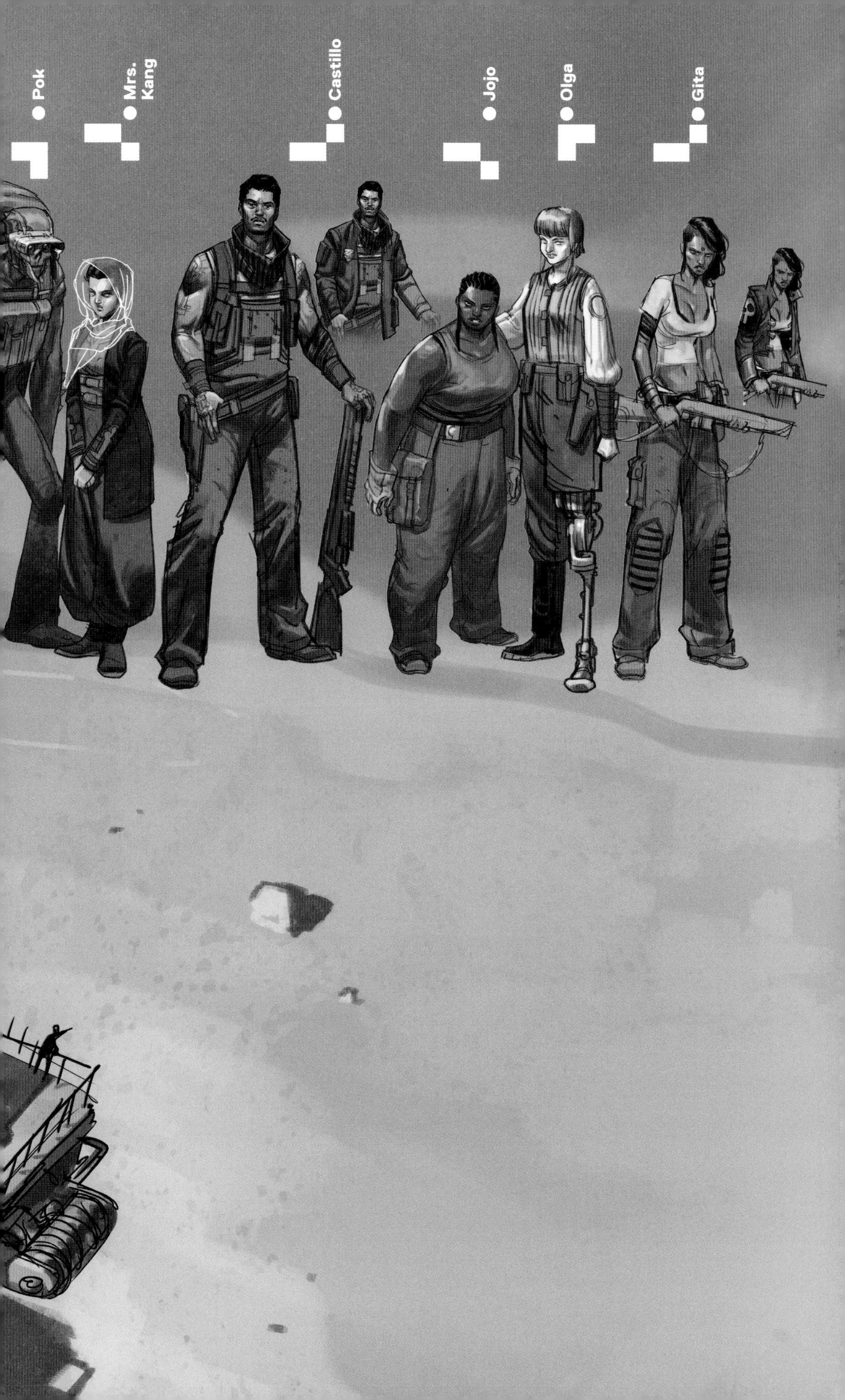

Pok
Mrs. Kang
Castillo
Jojo
Olga
Gita

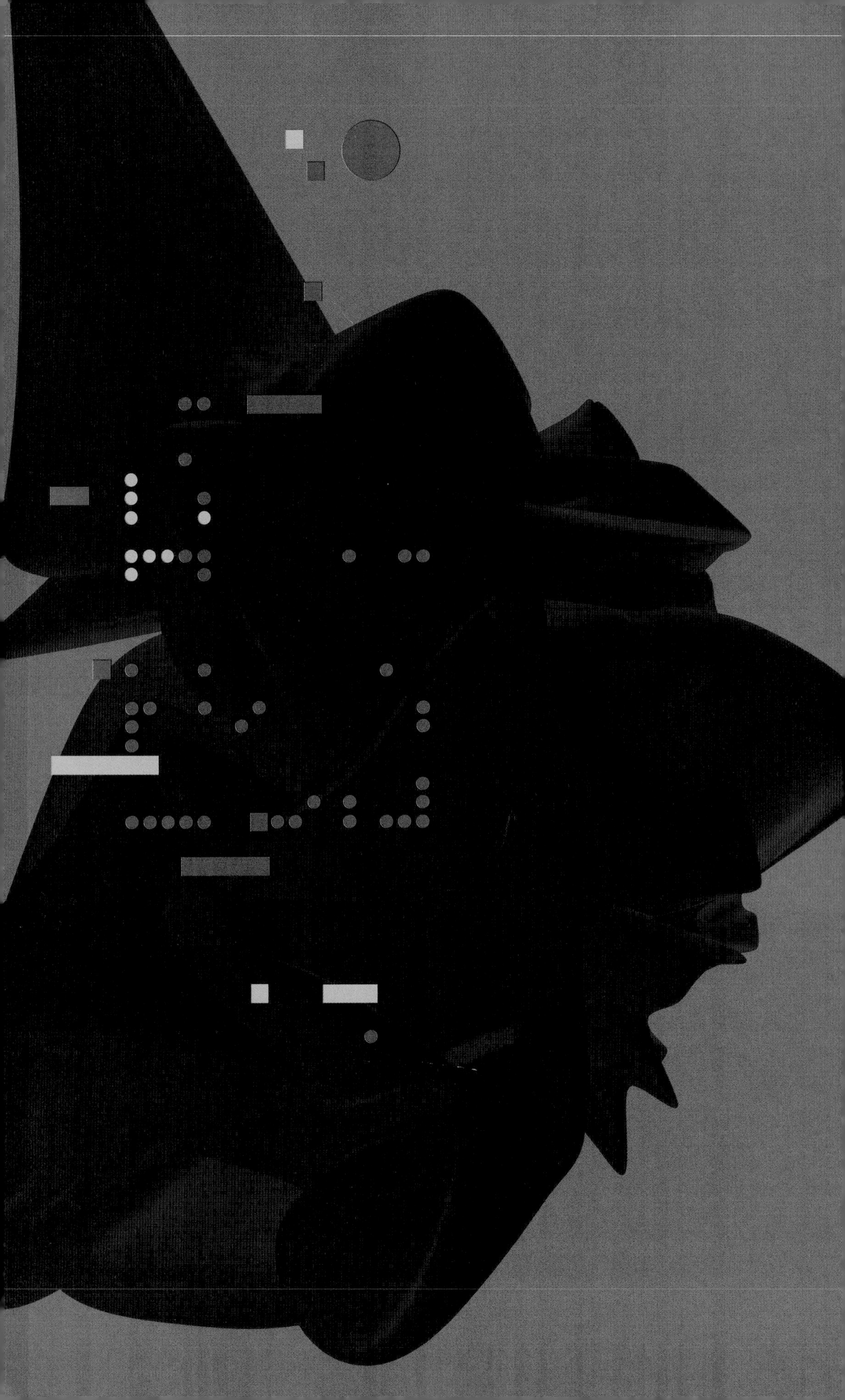

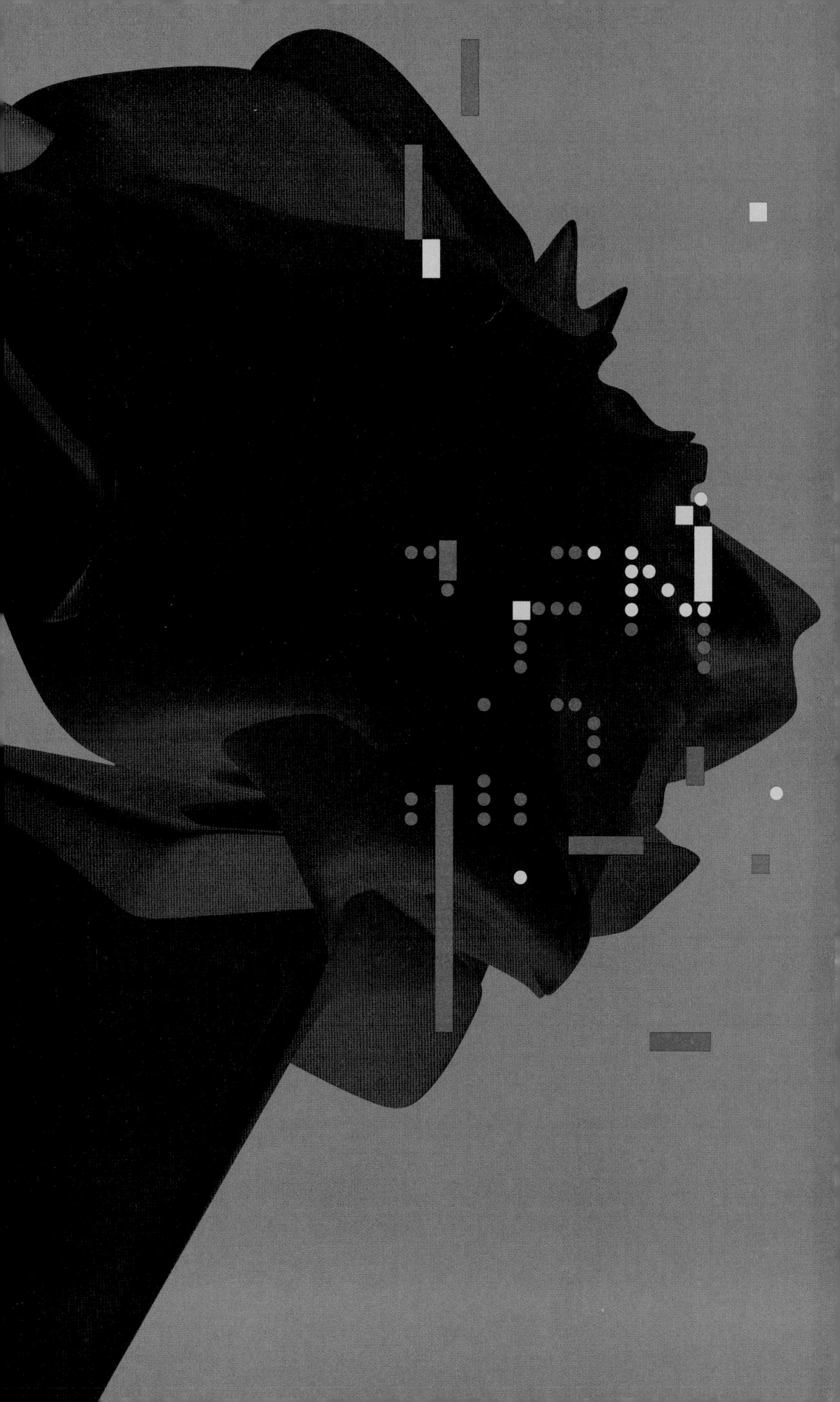

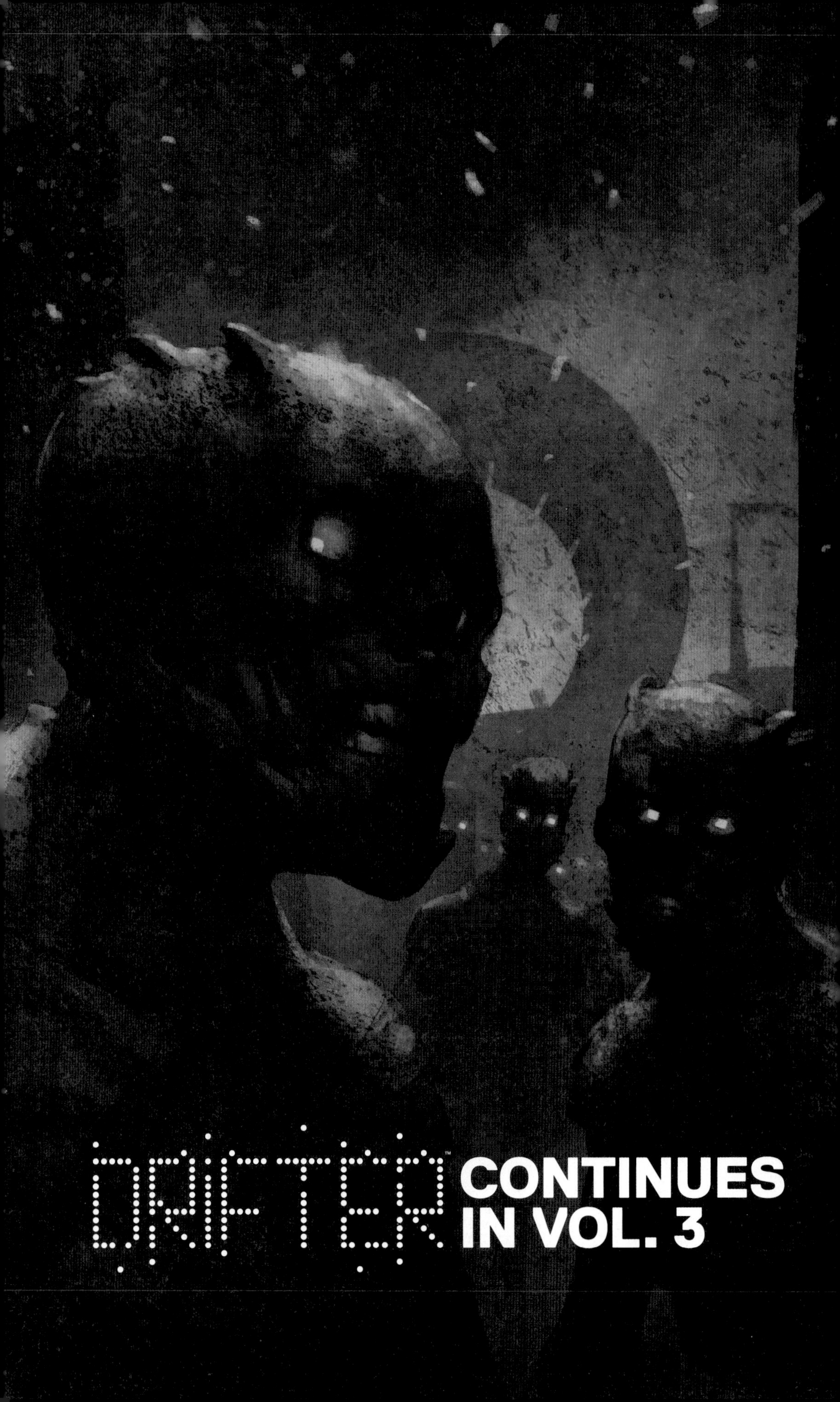
DRIFTER™ CONTINUES IN VOL. 3